Books by W. S. Merwin

POEMS

Travels 1993
The Second Four Books of Poems 1993
(INCLUDING THE COMPLETE TEXT OF
The Moving Target, The Lice, The Carrier of Ladders,
AND *Writings to an Unfinished Accompaniment*)
Selected Poems 1988
The Rain in the Trees 1988
Opening the Hand 1983
Finding the Islands 1982
The Compass Flower 1977
The First Four Books of Poems 1975
(INCLUDING THE COMPLETE TEXTS OF
A Mask for Janus, The Dancing Bears,
Green with Beasts AND *The Drunk in the Furnace*)
Writings to an Unfinished Accompaniment 1973
The Carrier of Ladders 1970
The Lice 1967
The Moving Target 1963
The Drunk in the Furnace 1960
Green with Beasts 1956
The Dancing Bears 1954
A Mask for Janus 1952

PROSE

The Lost Upland 1992
Unframed Originals 1982
Houses and Travellers 1977
The Miner's Pale Children 1970

TRANSLATIONS

From the Spanish Morning 1985
Four French Plays 1985
Selected Translations 1968–1978 1979
Osip Mandelstam, Selected Poems
(WITH CLARENCE BROWN) 1974
Asian Figures 1973
Transparence of the World (Poems by Jean Follain) 1969
Voices (Poems by Antonio Porchia) 1969, 1988
Products of the Perfected Civilization
(Selected Writings of Chamfort) 1969
Twenty Love Poems and a Song of Despair
(Poems by Pablo Neruda) 1969
Selected Translations 1948–1968 1968
The Song of Roland 1963
Lazarillo de Tormes 1962
Spanish Ballads 1961
The Satires of Persius 1960
The Poem of the Cid 1959

W. S. Merwin

THE
MINER'S
PALE
CHILDREN

An Owl Book
Henry Holt and Company
New York

Henry Holt and Company, Inc.
Publishers since 1866
115 West 18th Street
New York, New York 10011

Henry Holt® is a registered trademark
of Henry Holt and Company, Inc.

Published in Canada by Fitzhenry & Whiteside Ltd.,
195 Allstate Parkway, Markham, Ontario L3R 4T8.

Some of these pieces first appeared in The New Yorker, as follows: POSTCARDS
FROM THE MAGINOT LINE; THE WEDDING MARCH; THE FOUNTAIN; ETHEL'S
STORY; THE DEATH-DEFYING TORTONIS; THE VISITOR; THE REMEMBERING
MACHINES OF TOMORROW; THE CONQUEROR; THE LOCKER ROOM; A LOST
TRIBE; THE ROOFS; THE ABYSS; THE JUNE COUPLE; and THE FRAGMENTS.
Others appeared in the following magazines: Dragonfly, Field, Guabi, The
Iowa Review, Kayak, Lillabulero, New American Review, new work,
The New York Review of Books, Quarterly Review of Literature, The
Seneca Review, The Sumac Press, TriQuarterly, and Vortex.

Library of Congress Cataloging-in-Publication Data
Merwin, W. S. (William Stanley).
The miner's pale children / W. S. Merwin. — 1st Owl Book ed.
        p.   cm.
        I. Title.
PS3563.E75M5   1994   93-45574
811'54—dc20   CIP

ISBN 0-8050-2870-6

First published in hardcover in 1970 by Atheneum.

First Owl Book Edition—1994

Printed in the United States of America
All first editions are printed on acid-free paper. ∞

1   3   5   7   9   10   8   6   4   2

FOR MY MOTHER

Contents

Contents

Contents

Foreword to the 1994 Edition

ONE winter at the end of the sixties, I was living in New Mexico on the Old Santa Fe Trail at the edge of town. For a week or so I had been planning to go with friends to some ancient caves in the side of a mesa overlooking a valley, several hours away by car. But I had been sick with the flu for a few days, and when the morning came for the trip I had not recovered enough to be able to go. By then I had read what had been written about the cave and the area around it, and after my friends left I tried to imagine it. I began to write "The Dwelling," which became the first piece in *The Miner's Pale Children.* That writing seemed to open a gate I had not known was there, and others followed soon after. But I do not remember any plan for a book, any book at all. I had not given much consideration to writing prose pieces of the kind—whatever the kind is taken to be—and part of the excitement, when they did begin to occur, came from surprise.

I am still not certain what to call the pieces that took shape from that beginning, and almost at once this seemed to me a valuable condition, an advantage that I wanted to retain. I realized that I did not want these writings, if they ever came to comprise a substantial group, to qualify for membership in some recognizable genre. I hoped that they would keep raising some question about accepted boundaries and definitions of genres altogether. My own formal literary education had not accorded much regard to what in English are referred to as "prose poems," and I am not at all sure what that genre is supposed to entail. As I wrote, I was listening for recognizable but perhaps scarcely noticed or unacknowledged or emergent forms and conventions in current use. I recalled what I thought were precedents—fragments, essays, journal entries, instructions and lists, oral tales, fables. What I was hoping for as I went was akin to what made a poem seem complete. But it was prose that I was writing, and I was pleased when the pieces raised questions about the boundary between prose and poetry, and where we think it runs.

As the pieces continued to come I became aware that I was trying to touch and summon a dimension and a quality of expectation that we know from legends and from accounts that incorporate both familiarity and astonishment.

These pieces were born of their time in my own life and in the world I was inhabiting—a time when the hopes and liberations of the sixties were being challenged by war, ecological dismay, and political reaction. How the events of the time, public and private, influenced these fictions and the imagination they represent is something that I understood only in part even then, and I cannot pretend to know much about it now, even at a distance. But I am relieved when people talk to me about these writings as though they were contemporary, which is how they seem to me.

—W. S. Merwin
January 1994

The Miner's Pale Children

The Dwelling

Once when I looked at myself there was nothing. I could not see any size, any shape, any color. I could tell that I was still there because I was frightened, and I could feel that. When I began to think about myself it kept coming down to that, as though that was the only thing to remember. Yes, that was the only thing I could remember about myself clearly and accurately. I was frightened. That one thing went back until I vanished with it. The point of that disappearance could be considered a kind of beginning. And now to the original dread this new fear was added: that I might forget that I was afraid, and so vanish again, entirely.

The new fear was a revelation. It was, so to speak, an addition to my life and I might well have thought of it as a reason for indulging in a moment of precarious rejoicing. But oblivion never left my side. The more I learned the more terrible the possibilities appeared. When I grew too tired to stand up I leaned against a high smooth cliff that ran along a little valley. That way I had a wall at my back. I could tell that I had come to something that was used to staying.

The cliff faced south, across a small stream. The warmth of the day's sunlight remained in the stone after the sun went down. I went back to that place again and again. Because I was frightened I pressed myself against the stone like a being who wants to hide. Sometimes I really wanted to disappear into the cliff. In that one place I thought I might be able to vanish safely. Night after night I spent pressed against the smooth stone. One morning when I woke I saw my shape on it. It stayed there even when I moved away. It was a shadowy form, like the opening of a narrow mouth. I could see my color there on the wall. A kind of shallow darkness. The discovery came to me like a new fear, but I wanted to keep it. I decided not to leave. I spent all day at the cliff wall, pressed hard against it, deepening my shape on it, in my own mind. I even allowed a little of my fear to play at being hope. I stayed there day and night. The age of my wandering without a shape through the shadowy mountains began to seem very remote. A legend. A legend about myself. One day I could feel my appearance itself stirring on the cliff face, turning as the sun went through its course. I knew that my darkness on the wall had sunk into the stone and acquired a shadow of its own. Inside it.

Oblivion came then in the form of a messenger. Sometimes he called himself time, or water. But as soon as he appeared I set him to work. Whatever he told me I answered by becoming more myself. I pressed myself deep into the cliff, where the day never reached. He followed me in. We conversed in silence. At last there were chambers in me, like a heart. And the dust was marked with prints of presences, in the total dark. Some of them were his.

One day I was sure who I was. I left most of my fear in one dark chamber and began to extend outward from the cliff. A wall was built up to the overhanging stone. Other walls rose on either side, and my darkness moved in there, to stay. That day oblivion told me that he was my heir but I told him that I had made up my mind now, I would appear before I disappeared. Even if it made it worse. And I stood there, dark all the way to the outer wall built of separate stones, and was filled with the thought of what I was, and who.

I came to live more and more in the outer room. The inner chambers were a place apart. It seemed to me that the darkness was becoming solid in there. Some of my dreams went on sleeping in there, but places were found for them in the outer room, and in the end most of them moved out and stayed with me. But my fear still spent a great deal of time in there. And I still kept my back to the cliff.

Then one night I grew my own fourth wall, of separate stones. And a roof. Where the cliff had always been. The new stones were not to protect me. To free me. As the work went on I could feel a terrible tremor under me, a remote heaving such as runs through the earth around the roots of an old tree when the wind blows very hard. All of my fear came out of the cliff and joined me, leaving only a ghost of itself in the old place. When the sun rose I stood in the light with four walls. The mountains were far away and were still receding. The cliff was already out of sight. But I could see what I was. I was alone. I was waiting. I had a shadow outside me.

The days move past me now on every side. The birds fly all around me and plunge into the new distances behind me. I have added to the sky. The fear is the same as ever. It is safe now. Even when the roof falls and the walls collapse and the cliff is not even to be thought of and the daylight floods everything and I am forgotten, the fear will survive. Even if it cannot be seen its features will be known, and its existence will be in no doubt. It will be at home everywhere, like oblivion itself. I will not have lived in vain.

The Bar

I F YOU are at home in the bars of this country you will
be at home in this one. It seems to be simply one
more among so many others. No, no, this is the end of
seeming. It really is simply one more among so many
others.

The bar runs the full length of the room, from one
wall to another, with no curve at either end for a juke-
box or hat stand or telephone booth or entrance to the
bar or door to a rest room. But there is nothing abnormal
about that. The mirror runs all the way along the wall
behind the bar, from one end to the other. The bottles
are lined up against the mirror all the way, with that arrogance of slaves of an emperor, but that too is perfectly
ordinary. Most of the bar stools are occupied. Lighted
glass advertisements for beverages, hanging at intervals
from the ceiling, revolve slowly, stroking the occupants
with colored lights. Little beacons. Not real beacons, of
course. And on a box in a corner an illuminated panel
shows for a moment a young man and a young woman
shooting rapids in a canoe, in bright sunlight. The river
is very blue and they are smiling, holding up beer cans.
Then the scene changes and they are leaning on ski poles,

smiling and holding up beer cans. Then the scene changes again, but nobody watches. The line of backs at the bar faces outward like a ruined fortress. Perfectly normal.

Only when you have joined those on the stools will you notice at some point that at the end, where the bar arrives at the wall, the wall does not come all the way down to the bar top. There is a gap between, perhaps ten inches high, through which bottles, glasses, or other small objects could be passed. Through the opening the bar can be seen continuing beyond the wall. With drinks on it, and hands resting beside them, and little colored lights stroking them. Eventually you will manage to verify that at the other end of the room there is another such opening, with another glimpse of bar, drinks, hands, beyond it. Then you will notice that the doors marked EXIT are at either end of the room.

When someone new comes in a few of the backs straighten, and some of the heads turn. The newcomer stands for a moment embarrassed, afraid of disturbing something, silhouetted in the light of the illuminated scenes. Then he moves toward the bar as though to offer his poor services. When someone goes out through one of the doors at either end, no one pays any attention. The bar-keeper never speaks unless spoken to.

Beyond the bars on either side of this one there are others, and then others. The furnishings are the same, but the barmen have different faces. The illuminated scenes on the panels are different. People have their favorite haunts. They are conservative. To some it seems dangerous to move back and forth. And what for? The worst is having to go looking for someone else.

No ONE who was not born and brought up in them really knows of the life in the clothing drawers, and very few of those who did grow up there are willing to divulge any details of that ancient existence so close to our own, or as we like to say within our own, and yet so unfamiliar. No, they answer, everything has been taken from us from the beginning and you have given us only what you chose to, with no concern for us. What essentials remain to us, the secrets of our life, we will keep to ourselves. If our way of life is doomed as a result of yours, its secrets will die with it, and its meaning. We will not lend those to you for your masquerades.

By now scholars have tried everything to bring those secrets to the light of present-day reality, and with almost no success. Devices for opening the drawers suddenly have revealed nothing but the contents lying like the dead whom the light suddenly surprises. Cameras with flash-bulbs, left in the drawers in houses where no one was staying, and timed to go off during the darkest and most silent hours, have disclosed still more eerie vistas of inert recumbency; always the life has remained cloaked in the motionless forms. Electronic recording devices rigged in the same manner have picked up nothing but the gradual sinking into sleep of consciousness after consciousness in the house, until at last only one alien witness remained awake: the recorder was registering its own unrewarded vigil. It has been claimed that these last results, nevertheless, represent a step forward. If not a record of the life itself, at least they supply a record of the outer world from that life's point of view.

As might have been expected, most of the few sources of information on this life so turned away from our own have come from milieux in which neglect in one form or another has already advanced its work. Loose garments, tossed in unfolded, perhaps uncleaned, long ago, and abandoned to their own shapes have not always been able to conceal the evidences of a life to which they were born and which they had almost forgotten the need to hide. A darkness from their own world, and an odor of it, clings to them here and there when they are too abruptly hauled into ours. Others that once existed as pairs and have lost their consorts, stray buttons, fragments of ornamentation, demoralized and with a weakened sense of the future, perhaps, also betray at times the existence of other mores, other values, other hopes, if not those things themselves. These are not ideal witnesses, perhaps, but is there any such thing?

At any rate it is hard to sort out probability from sectarian wishful thinking, in the scant testimony thus gathered. The witnesses suggest that their own order of things, its darkness, its anticipation in which time plays no part, its community without sound, its dances, its dances, whatever they may be, are part of an order that is older than the cupboards and will survive them. They also infer quite calmly that the world of uses, for which they were fashioned and in which they are worn, knows almost nothing of reality.

The Basilica of the Scales

THERE is disagreement about the dates of each phase of the present edifice. No one can establish incontravertibly when the first primitive chapel was constructed on this site. Parts of the crypt survive from that earliest place of worship. Massive squat squared pillars of gray stone. Medals and military decorations of a later day have been affixed to them on all sides like cloaks, and glitter in the light of the votive candles. The church has been rebuilt at least three times, incorporating the designs and proportions of successive ages. Each time it has been considerably enlarged. The facade has moved west. It is from there that we enter. From farther away. The transept has broadened like the canyon of a gray river flowing between us and the chancel. Most important of all, each time the ceiling, the ceiling has risen.

It cannot be seen. Not from anywhere in the basilica. All that meets the eye when one looks up, wherever one is, are the scales. Like leaves they hang everywhere above the worshippers and the curious. They are suspended at all heights, from those that can barely be descried through the pans and chains of others lower down, to a few which seem to be almost within reach—an illusion caused by some trick of perspective, as one discovers if one finds oneself near them. They are of all sizes, from delicate brass instruments such as apothecaries still use, to vast measures with pans that a heavy man could stand in, beams thicker than an arm and longer, and chains in proportion. And they too are of all ages. Some of them, it is said, are older, much older, than the first building itself. They were brought from far away and their origins are legendary like that of the grail. But none of them belong to our accounts any longer. No one climbs to examine them.

And it would be unthinkable to take one down. In the course of the many centuries since the last building was finished, two or three have fallen. One can imagine the terror that swept through the devout who were present when one of the silent measures suspended above them suddenly detached itself, with a sound of metal snapping and groaning, from what had seemed its everlasting equilibrium, and had crashed down through the lower choirs of chains and hammered pans, setting up a clangor of cymbals, a rocking and lamentation that left the farthest scales in the remote ceiling swinging and vibrating with dying songs. The fallen measures lay like dead supplicants on the granite floor. No one touched them. No one was sure what they meant. No one knelt to pray near them on the bare stone unless the crowd of worshippers pressed them closer than they would have chosen to be. In time iron railings were erected around the collapsed measures where they lay. Black cloth was draped from the rail and removed only between the evening of Good Friday and Easter morning. Candles—not votive lights but thick columns of wax the color of the faces of the dead—flickered perpetually at the corners of the enclosures.

As for the scales suspended above, it would be hard to say at a glance whether they are still or moving. A distant quiet hangs in the pans like dust. And yet the eye that remains fixed upon them for some time detects, or seems to detect, a scarcely perceptible motion, such as we think we see if we stare for long at the faces of the dead. And in fact the scales are at all times in motion. Often it is so slight that the unaided eye could not discern it at all if it were not that the thousands of minute swayings all cast shadows into the thickets of chains, beams, pans, and the shadows magnify the movements, giving that impression of a breathing lost in itself. Occasionally a single balance will forsake its equilibrium, without apparent warning, and one of its pans will slowly sink farther and farther as the other rises, then even more slowly right itself. The phenomenon has fostered various explanations. Some say it is due to a death. Some ascribe it to a peculiar fervor of prayer. Others declare that it is the dove descending. Or a wind. Past, present, or to come.

Tergvinder's Stone

ONE time my friend Tergvinder brought a large round boulder into his living room. He rolled it up the steps with the help of some two-by-fours, and when he got it out into the middle of the room, where some people have coffee tables (though he had never had one there himself) he left it. He said that was where it belonged.

It is really a plain-looking stone. Not as large as Plymouth Rock by a great deal, but then it does not have all the claims of a big shaky promotion campaign to support. That was one of the things Tergvinder said about it. He made no claims at all for it, he said. It was other people who called it Tergvinder's Stone. All he said was that according to him it belonged there.

His dog took to peeing on it, which created a problem (Tergvinder had not moved the carpet before he got the stone to where he said it belonged). Their tomcat took to squirting it, too. His wife fell over it quite often at first and it did not help their already strained marriage. Tergvinder said there was nothing to be done about it. It was in the order of things. That was a phrase he seldom employed, and never when he conceived that there was any room left for doubt.

He confided in me that he often woke in the middle of the night, troubled by the ancient, nameless ills of the planet, and got up quietly not to wake his wife, and walked through the house naked, without turning on any lights. He said that at such times he found himself listening, listening, aware of how some shapes in the darkness emitted low sounds like breathing, as they never did by day. He said he had become aware of a hole in the darkness in the middle of the living room, and out of that hole a breathing, a mournful dissatisfied sound of an absence waiting for what belonged to it, for something it had never seen and could not conceive of, but without which it could not rest. It was a sound, Tergvinder said, that touched him with fellow-feeling, and he had undertaken—oh, without saying anything to anybody—to assuage, if he could, that wordless longing that seemed always on the verge of despair. How to do it was another matter, and for months he had circled the problem, night and day, without apparently coming any closer to a solution. Then one day he had seen the stone. It had been there all the time at the bottom of his drive, he said, and he had never really seen it. Never recognized it for what it was. The nearer to the house he had got it, the more certain he had become. The stone had rolled into its present place like a lost loved one falling into arms that had long ached for it.

Tergvinder says that now on nights when he walks through the dark house he comes and stands in the living room doorway and listens to the peace in the middle of the floor. He knows its size, its weight, the touch of it, something of what is thought of it. He knows that it is peace. As he listens, some hint of that peace touches him too. Often, after a while, he steps down into the living room and goes and kneels beside the stone and they converse for hours in silence—a silence broken only by the sound of his own breathing.

The Dachau Shoe

M Y COUSIN Gene (he's really only a second cousin) has a shoe he picked up at Dachau. It's a pretty worn-out shoe. It wasn't top quality in the first place, he explained. The sole is cracked clear across and has pulled loose from the upper on both sides, and the upper is split at the ball of the foot. There's no lace and there's no heel.

He explained he didn't steal it because it must have belonged to a Jew who was dead. He explained that he wanted some little thing. He explained that the Russians looted everything. They just took anything. He explained that it wasn't top quality to begin with. He explained that the guards or the kapos would have taken it if it had been any good. He explained that he was lucky to have got anything. He explained that it wasn't wrong because the Germans were defeated. He explained that everybody was picking up something. A lot of guys wanted flags or daggers or medals or things like that, but that kind of thing didn't appeal to him so much. He kept it on the mantelpiece for a while but he explained that it wasn't a trophy.

He explained that it's no use being vindictive. He ex-

plained that he wasn't. Nobody's perfect. Actually we
share a German grandfather. But he explained that this
was the reason why we had to fight that war. What happened at Dachau was a crime that could not be allowed
to pass. But he explained that we could not really do
anything to stop it while the war was going on because
we had to win the war first. He explained that we
couldn't always do just what we would have liked to do.
He explained that the Russians killed a lot of Jews too.
After a couple of years he put the shoe away in a
drawer. He explained that the dust collected in it.

Now he has it down in the cellar in a box. He explains
that the central heating makes it crack worse. He'll show
it to you, though, any time you ask. He explains how it
looks. He explains how it's hard to take it in, even for
him. He explains how it was raining, and there weren't
many things left when he got there. He explains how
there wasn't anything of value and you didn't want to
get caught taking anything of that kind, even if there
had been. He explains how everything inside smelled. He
explains how it was just lying out in the mud, probably
right where it had come off. He explains that he ought to
keep it. A thing like that.

You really ought to go and see it. He'll show it to you.
All you have to do is ask. It's not that it's really a very
interesting shoe when you come right down to it but
you learn a lot from his explanations.

Make This Simple Test

BLINDFOLD yourself with some suitable object. If time permits remain still for a moment. You may feel one or more of your senses begin to swim back toward you in the darkness, singly and without their names. Meanwhile have someone else arrange the products to be used in a row in front of you. It is preferable to have them in identical containers, though that is not necessary. Where possible, perform the test by having the other person feed you a portion—a spoonful—of each of the products in turn, without comment.

Guess what each one is, and have the other person write down what you say.

Then remove the blindfold. While arranging the products the other person should have detached part of the label or container from each and placed it in front of the product it belongs to, like a title. This bit of legend must not contain the product's trade name nor its generic name, nor any suggestion of the product's taste or desirability. Or price. It should be limited to that part of the label or container which enumerates the actual components of the product in question.

Thus, for instance:

"Contains dextrinized flours, cocoa processed with alkali, non-fat dry milk solids, yeast nutrients, vegetable proteins, agar, hydrogenated vegetable oil, dried egg yolk, GUAR, sodium cyclamate, soya lecithin, imitation lemon oil, acetyl tartaric esters of mono- and diglycerides as emulsifiers, polysorbate 60, $\frac{1}{10}$ of 1% of sodium benzoate to retard spoilage."

Or:

"Contains anhydrated potatoes, powdered whey, vegetable gum, emulsifier (glycerol monostearate), invert syrup, shortening with freshness preserver, lactose, sorbic acid to retard mold growth, caramel color, natural and artificial flavors, sodium acid pyrophosphate, sodium bisulfite."

Or:

"Contains beef extract, wheat and soya derivatives, food starch-modified, dry sweet whey, calcium carageenan, vegetable oil, sodium phosphates to preserve freshness, BHA, BHT, prophylene glycol, pectin, niacinamide, artificial flavor, U.S. certified color."

There should be not less than three separate products.

Taste again, without the blindfold. Guess again and have the other person record the answers. Replace the blindfold. Have the other person change the order of the products and again feed you a spoonful of each.

Guess again what you are eating or drinking in each case (if you can make the distinction.) But this time do not stop there. Guess why you are eating or drinking it. Guess what it may do for you. Guess what it was meant to do for you. By whom. When. Where. Why. Guess where in the course of evolution you took the first step toward it. Guess which of your organs recognize it. Guess whether it is welcomed to their temples. Guess how it figures in their prayers. Guess how completely you become what you eat. Guess how soon. Guess at the taste of locusts and wild honey. Guess at the taste of water. Guess what the rivers see as they die. Guess why the babies are burning. Guess why there is silence in heaven. Guess why you were ever born.

Postcards from the Maginot Line

THIS morning there was another one in the mail. A slightly blurred and clumsily retouched shot of some of the fortifications, massive and scarcely protruding from the enormous embankments. The guns—the few that can be seen—look silly, like wax cigars. The flag looks like a lead soldier's, with the paint put on badly. The whole thing might be a model.

But there have been the others. Many of them. For the most part seen from the exterior, from all angles—head-on, perspectives facing north and facing south, looking out from the top of the embankments, even one from above. They might all have been taken from a model, in fact, but when they are seen together that impression fades. And then there are the interiors. Officers' quarters which, the legend says, are hundreds of feet below ground. Views of apparently endless corridors into which little ramps of light descend at intervals; panels of dials of different sizes, with black patches on them that have been censored out. It was rather startling to notice a small flicker of relief at the sight of the black patches: it had seemed somehow imprudent to make public display of so much of the defenses.

A few of the cards have shown other, related subjects: a mezzotint of Maginot as a child in the 1880's, a
view of the house where he grew up, with his portrait
in an oval inset above it, pictures of villages near the line
of fortifications, with their churches, and old men sitting under trees, and cows filing through the lanes, and
monuments from other wars. They have all been marked,
front and back, in heavy black letters THE MAGINOT
LINE, and the legend in each case has made the relation
clear. And the postmarks are all from there.

They have been coming for months, at least once a
week. All signed simply "Pierre." Whoever he is. He
certainly seems to know me, or know about me—referring to favorite authors, incidents from my childhood,
friends I have not seen for years. He says repeatedly that
he is comfortable there. He praises what he calls the
tranquillity of the life. He says, as though referring to an
old joke, that with my fondness for peace I would like
it. He says war is unthinkable. A thing of the past. He
describes the flowers in the little beds. He describes the
social life. He tells what he is reading. He asks why I
never write. He asks why none of us ever write. He says
we have nothing to fear.

The Weight of Sleep

AT THE very mention of it there is one kind of person who laughs or looks away. You know at once where he is—in his life, in the story of the species, in the adventure of the planet. For the weight of sleep cannot be measured. By definition, some might say, though has it ever been defined? At least it cannot be measured by any scale known to the perspectives of waking. Presumably it might be measured one day if machines were contrived that resembled us so closely that they slept. And required sleep. But there again, can we tell how they would differ from us? How their sleep would differ from ours? There again one reaches for definitions and touches darkness.

And yet the weight of sleep is one of the only things that we know. We have been aware of it since we knew anything, since the first moment after conception. It grew with us, it grows along with us, it draws us on. Its relation to the gravity of the planet is merely one of analogy. The weight of sleep draws us back inexorably toward a unity that is entirely ours but that we cannot possess, that resembles the sky itself as much as it does the centers of the heavenly bodies.

When did it begin? With life itself? Long before? Or a little time after, when consciousness, the whole of consciousness, scarcely begun, suddenly became aware of itself like a caught breath, and was seized with panic and longing and the knowledge of travail? Yes, it was then that the weight of sleep came to it, the black angel full of promises. With different forms for each life. Different dances.

For the planet itself it was simpler. To the whole of the globe's first life as it became conscious of itself, everything seemed to have stopped in the terrible light. Everything stood in the grip of the single command: Weariness. Forever and ever. Then came the black angel.

For the planet his shape can be pictured as that of a driving wheel of a locomotive. The rim is darkness; he is always present. The spokes are darkness. They divide the light, though they disappear as they turn. They meet at the center. The hub is darkness. Across one side is a segment of solid black. There is the weight of sleep, properly speaking: its throne. There the wheel's mass preserves its motion. There its stillness dreams of falling. There what it is dreams of what it is.

Our Jailer

OUR jailer is in the habit of placing a baited mouse trap in the cells of the condemned on their last night. Ours is a well-kept jail; mice are rare and not many stray into the occupied cells. The jailer watches the prisoners.

Surprisingly few, he says, remain completely indifferent to the presence of the trap throughout the whole night. A larger number become absorbed by it and sit staring at it, whether or not it occupies their thoughts consistently. A proportion which he has recorded releases the trap, either at once or after a period of varying length. He has other statistics for those who deliberately smash the trap, those who move it (presumably to a more likely spot), those who make a mark on the wall if a mouse is caught in the trap, and those who make one if none was caught, either to state the fact or to bequeath, as a tiny triumph, a lie.

Month after month, year after year, he watches them. And we watch him. And each other.

Shine on, Tottering Republic

I N THE last days of the presidents a new star appeared. By then the organization of fear was vast and persuasive beyond anything that could have been conceived by the founding fathers. It involved the whole economy. Every coin, changing hands, paid tribute to it. The rings of warning and defense, whether or not they were penetrable, insured that the entire planet would be pulverized in the event of an attack or the appearance of one. On the domestic front the police were their own masters, and no branch of technology was closed to them. Any window, any light bulb, any picture might be a television camera connected to the nearest precinct. No one dared to examine too closely. Those who did might be arrested a few minutes later, charged with obstruction or conspiracy. Bail no longer existed, trials came seldom, sentences were inevitable, heavy, and without appeal. On the whole, it was said, the public was relieved at the steady disappearance of disturbing elements.

Then the star appeared. On the dollar, first. On the seal, in the circular array above the motto E PLURIBUS UNUM (FROM MANY ONE) bill after bill began to show one star too many. It gave the motto new possibilities, but that was scarcely noticed. There were some arrests for counterfeiting but the scandal spread rapidly and involved several large banks. Severity was recommended as the number of bills that had to be withdrawn grew from edition to edition of the daily papers. Possession of the improper bills was harshly dealt with. Then for a few days the media were silent on the subject and only the pressure of rumor forced the government to admit at last that the offending constellation had been traced back to the mint itself. But the die that had wrought the terrible addition was not found. And when new bills were issued, within a week notes with the same serial numbers, and otherwise indistinguishable by any known techniques, contained the new star. The search for the counterfeiters surpassed any hunt in the nation's history. Suspect after suspect was seized, grilled, tried, sentenced, publicized, but the star continued to appear. At last the bill was completely withdrawn, and redesigned without the seal.

Then the star began appearing on the flag. Again it was simply embarrassing at first. No one could understand how it came to be there: one too many in one of the rows, not always the same row. It happened on flags that people had owned for years. Sometimes it seemed to occur overnight, to patriots who were accustomed to hoisting their flags every morning. Some were mortified and then frightened, at the thought that they might have flown the improper constellation for a day or even more without noticing it, and that someone else might have counted. For by then everyone counted, all the time. Less and less flags were flown.

In time there was no piece of the national insignia that did not risk the appearance of the free, illegal star. Officers' uniforms, taken from cupboards in their own homes, would prove to have acquired the shameful decoration through no agency known to the owners. Medals locked in cases displayed the unwarranted distinction when the cases were opened. Document after document affixed with the seal turned out to be of questionable validity because the new star had found them with its mark. Even on those monuments to the war dead that bore stars it appeared again and again under the final name, with a blank space after it. A few days later there would be another one. Followed by a blank. And then another. And another.

At last the flag was re-designed. With no stars at all. The seal was re-designed. Without stars. All the national insignia were re-designed without stars. All the stars were chiselled from the monuments to the war dead. And the country shook itself, not without suspicion but not without a smile, and began to recover from its shame.

Memory

I N THE first place is it a virtue after all? We despise
those who are deficient in it, but that may be nothing but our predilection for those deceits that have hood-
winked us in particular, and our devotion to the habits
into which they have led us. We pretend to think it is
reasonable because it has taught us to reason. We pretend to believe that it is the guardian of wisdom, an an-
tique ornament which it has shown us on favored occasions lying in a velvet box that we are to inherit some
day if we are good.

On the other hand, like the rest of the blindfolded
deities, it is a source of terrible arrogance. It persuades
us that nothing of the past remains except what we remember. From there it is only a step to persuading us
that the present too would be meaningless without it.
And we take that step moment by moment as though
the light fell nowhere else.

So to say that we would not be here, or even to ask
indulgently what we would be, without it, proves nothing. Except that most of what we call our virtues have
been made of necessities by processes that we later tried
to forget. What does that tell us about our bondage?

See, the sailor emerges at last from the loom. He is convinced that his guide through all the weavings has been a personification of wisdom itself. And so memory, he repeats as he paces the familiar shore, has played no tricks on him. His guide had told him that things would look smaller, that the dogs would be old and the eyes milky. No, he says, due allowance having been made for the passage of time (as he has been careful to do) it is just as he remembered it. The same shadows on the same walls, the same lines and the same unimpressed absence on the hills. If he thought he detected a slight echo to his voice in the first moments it was gone by the time he listened for it. Even the unpleasant details—the screaming of one of the local hysterics, the smell of the back premises of the port, the crabbed features of a neighbor, the resumption of insoluble disputes and onerous responsibilities, were exactly as he had remembered them. He told himself that he had sweetened nothing, that he had been just.

Then why, by the third day—the day of resurrections—this bewilderment, this sense of being utterly lost, of turning, without a goal, in a great emptiness that, for all he knew, reached to the end of the world? Here was something that he had not remembered. Something that he never seemed to be able to remember. That same oppression that he had endured so often in this very place, that he had left with anguish and relief and now recognized with a stunned dread. What could he call it? His own presence in the place? The standing on the needle? The present? The blankness at the end of the story.

The Wedding March

To BE honest it was really too late when we started
out to look for the United Fish and Fowl Shipping
Company Restaurant, and not the kind of evening that
would have been best for such an expedition. The sun
had gone down without calling attention to itself. The
twilight had had a greenish cast to it that stayed on in the
streets. The air was heavy and dank. On the sidewalk
somebody said that it would be too much trouble to rain.

It seemed knowledgeable to have heard of the United
Fish and Fowl Shipping Company Restaurant, to mention it casually as a possibility. It's a Japanese raw fish
and chicken restaurant, very cheap. The party had been
pretty dreadful but we were happy. It was quite early to
be leaving a party although it was really too late to be
starting out looking for the restaurant. I explained that
although I had been there as a child I couldn't be said to
know that part of town at all well. I should say I didn't
know it at all. Some nice people were going to come
with us, but in the end they didn't.

It takes quite a long time to get out there. That's one
of the disadvantages. Then at last we were in the neigh-

borhood. Empty streets. They hadn't even taken up the old street-car tracks. Big warehouses on both sides, and a few wholesalers tucked among them, dusty and closed. All the doors looked like garage doors. I had a little map a friend had drawn for me. How to get there from the subway. It was on a side street. Nothing seemed to live there but cats. I saw a sign that looked as though it said United Fish and Fowl Shipping Company Restaurant down along the bend of the street, but wasn't sure. Before we got close enough to read it, we noticed a cop, in a car. He had drawn up to make a note. He had stopped in back of us, but I went back to ask him if he knew where the United Fish and Fowl Shipping Company Restaurant was.

Actually he had rather a pleasant face. He wasn't very old. He was polite. Though you never can tell. He was writing in a little notebook. He didn't answer or look up right away. He said yes, that was the place. Then he looked at me as though I were a high-school student and he were a high-school teacher who knew something about me. He said we didn't really want to go to that restaurant, did we? I explained that we'd been told about it. He asked who told us. I said a friend. He gave a little laugh. He said where we ought to go was the Chinese restaurant around the corner on the main street. He said we'd like that better. It would be a better place for us. Then I thought, I suppose now he'll watch to see which one we head for. But he said he was really off duty and on his way home. It was true, it was a private car. It was a big favor he'd been doing me. But that didn't mean that he owed me anything. He'd made it clear. I said good-night and he drove off.

We couldn't believe the restaurant. It looked more like a store-front church. The windows were painted on the inside, all the way up, with a little chipped black and gold frieze, probably a decal, along the top. The color of the paint must have been what they call Ivory but in that light it looked the shade of dried peas. There was a street light farther down the block, near enough so that you could read the sign, lettered in dark red, and through the chipped places in the frieze you could see that there was a bulb lit inside too. On one side of the restaurant a passage was boarded up and had another sign on it, a warning. On the other side there was a big sign about an elevator shaft. Inside the restaurant there were voices, Japanese probably, and sounds of tables or crates thudding and banging. We discussed it and decided to try the Chinese place after all.

It was quite near. The stores on the street were closed, even the drug-store, but the Chinese restaurant was still open. When we went in there was no one at the tables. A Chinese man of middle years and girth who seemed as though he might be the proprietor came from the back, smiling and greeting, smelling of soap. He said it wasn't too late, but then he went and locked the door behind us, and drew the curtains. There were other people in the kitchen or the back rooms. You could hear them banging metal around and laughing. He waited among the tables and took our order. I asked him whether he had heard of a Japanese Restaurant called the United Fish and Fowl Shipping Company Restaurant and he said he had. I asked him whether it was good and he said it was. Then he left us.

He brought part of the order and then he was gone for a good while. The banging and laughing stopped in the back, there was a shuffling, the voices dropped and grew more serious. Just as he reappeared with the rest of the order there was a sound of a clarinet or some other wood-wind instrument warming up, and a stringed instrument being tuned. He was smiling as though a great joke were being prepared and we were in on it. Or were part of it. A head popped out from the kitchen, looked at us, a hand covered its mouth to hide a giggle. Then it disappeared. He left us again.

Suddenly from the back came the music. Something from Schubert first. A bit brassy and quite loud, with more drum than usual, and a tambourine. Then the *Largo* from Xerxes. And finally the *Wedding March* from Lohengrin, over and over. Over and over, until we had finished, and the tea was gone, and we needed more. The man reappeared to see how we were doing. Smiling at the same joke. As he took the tea pot I asked him if there was a wedding.

Yes, he said. There was a wedding. A wedding.

I asked him where.

He shrugged. "Somewhere," he said.

When?

"Every night," he said. "We play."

And you could see that it was true. Every night somewhere there is a wedding. The guests gather. The procession begins. The groom's party advances, and the groom. The bride's party, and the bride. They are united, they file out together, the guests crowd after them. All in silence. While the music is being played there. There in the locked Chinese restaurant, in the back room.

Spiders I Have Known

THE ONE no bigger than the head of a pencil, that emerged from the forehead of the new dentist perhaps an inch above his left eyebrow, ran down to the eyebrow and along it and dropped from the side of his face to the little scalloped glass tray on which the dentist was selecting a drill. It then disappeared. From my sight at least. I did not wish to call the dentist's attention to it at that precise moment. Besides I recognized that it was a perfectly harmless variety.

I would have been ashamed to be afraid.

The one that I found had taken up residence in a bundle of letters only a few months old. It was smaller than the wolf spiders that live in some of the corners and do no harm at all. It was also darker than they, and heavily—beautifully—furred. Some of its children clung to it like troops of tiny dust-colored anthropoids, and others had taken up lodgings in several of the larger envelopes. I looked up the species. Its bite is not poisonous, if I identified it correctly. I devoted some time to trying to remember which letters those were, who had written them, what they had said, whether I had answered them, and how things now stood, as a result, with each of the correspondents.

I would have been afraid to be ashamed.

The one that hung in the old apple tree that spring when we returned at last to the farm by the lake with its old garden into which I had been allowed to run, alone, with only a perfunctory word of caution from my mother, a word whose real purpose had been to dispel the attention of my father. The blossoms were just opening on the tree and the air rushed past me carrying them with it as though I were on a swing, when suddenly there it was in front of me, as big as my face, against the bright sky the color and depth of the fenders of the new car. The whole web was swaying gently in the wind. The abdomen had a kind of face on it. No, not a face, a mask. In orange and yellow. I knew it was a kind that was more afraid of me than I was of it.

I was ashamed.

The one that ran across each of my footprints in turn as I was crossing the dry bit on my way back, when you were sick and we didn't know how it would go after that, but maybe it wasn't working at all. I had the medicines but not much faith in them. It came to the edge of each footprint, hesitated, and then shot across like a woman with a baby, afraid of snipers, or a good child caught in a cloudburst. I couldn't understand how it kept up with me. My hands were full. You were in pain. I didn't want to stop. It's bad luck to harm them. Poor things. Besides, the danger of that species has been greatly exaggerated.

I would have been ashamed.

The Fountain

I N THE forest of Morb, which means untouched, there
is a fountain known as Llorndy, which means unchanging. The forest stretches for many days' ride over
the plateau. Other trees must have grown there once.
Now there are none but the oaks. They are immense,
and everywhere. There are no clearings. The forest is so
tall and dense that no birds live in it except owls and the
little wren that can make her way through the unlit veins
of the earth to its heart and find nourishment on the way.
The bird of the goddess of wisdom, who cannot find her
mistress. And the bird of the sovereign of darkness, who
sings to herself. No one lives in the forest. No building
will stand. Springs well up wherever one stone is placed
on another, and the walls topple and sink into the earth
before they can be said to be walls. No roads cross the
forest. Water emerges from them before they have been
laid, and they become long deepening quagmires. No
paths cross the forest. Even fresh paths of deer and badg-
ers grow old after a few yards and then vanish as though
the undergrowth or the bed of leaves had never been disturbed. No one hunts here. The owl and the wren follow intruders, calling out wherever they go. There is no

other voice, except their echoes. The oaks are so high that the rustling of the leaves cannot be heard from the ground, but the murmur seems to prevent any other vibration from entering. Only around the fountain of Llorndy and along its little stream of sweet water is there a continuous thread of sound.

The fountain emerges from a large rock on a gentle slope. A piece of pale gray stone, limestone, though the rocks in the forest and in the piled mounds of stone around it are granite or basalt or slate. Its pallor is startling, as though it were a faint light among the dark vegetation. It rises in a vaguely conical shape, with two columns down the front and the green stain between them where the water flows to begin the stream. The shape of an animal, seated erect, with no head. At the level of the collar the water wells out and brims over, blind, tireless, unchanging.

Once the forest was a great kingdom, rich and beautiful. Its farms were well-stocked and peaceful. Its arts were old and sure. Its borders were safe. It was on good terms with its neighbors. It was ruled by a king who was cultivated, intelligent, kind, and beloved of his subjects and of his family. But he was not happy, because he had a hard heart. He knew it. He had tried everything: women and religion, the company of children, the contemplation of flowers, the presence of animals, the sky itself, and he loved them all but he could tell that his heart was still hard. He loved them, he confessed to himself, only because he could imagine that they were his. And his heart remained as it was.

When his secret had been weighing on him for several years, the kingdom began to suffer from drought. In spring and autumn, when rain normally fell plentifully, the clouds gathered as usual but less and less rain fell every year, and in some years there was almost none. The summers lengthened and were less and less relieved by showers. The winters were moistened only by condensation and the humors remaining in the earth. New wells were dug but they ran dry almost at once. Dams were made but their water seeped away into cracked mud. The pastures grew bare; the farms were hungry. One by one, family by family, the inhabitants of the kingdom asked permission to leave. The king was kind and granted it, without exception, giving each family some present as it left, and provisions for the journey —dry provisions, and even a supply of precious water. Some were too ashamed to ask, and left without a word. The kingdom grew emptier as the months passed, and drier. The king sat in his darkened throne room. He had hung the walls with mourning. The windows were smoked, the columns and the candles were painted black. It was painful for him to converse with anyone, including his family. He knew that the kingdom was suffering this misfortune because his own heart was hard.

"And if only my heart were not as hard as it is," he said to the black columns, "I would know what to do. Should I go away? Is there any reason to imagine that that would solve the matter? As long as my heart is hard, this which is the result of it will go on. Furthermore it was here that it grew hard. Being somewhere else will not change it. If it is to be changed it had best be changed here, or else I will never be sure.

"Should I die? But what difference would that make? If I died with a hard heart would anything be changed? Everything might very well go on just as it is.

"Should I abdicate? It would make no difference. My own hard heart brought about this revulsion in nature. There is no way I can leave that behind. Even if I went and lived in a shepherd's hut, out on the plateau where the sheep have all died of starvation or thirst, my heart would be the same, and so nothing would change."

One day an animal came to see the king. He had never

seen an animal like that one. It was larger than a horse, but was shaped more like a dog. Its eyes were set so deep in its head that he could not see them at all. They seemed to be nothing but holes. The animal was covered with long pale fur, almost white, and had a thick tail, and paws like a cat's. The claws clicked on the darkened stone floor of the throne room. The creature came close to the black candle burning in front of the throne although it was broad day outside, and there it greeted him.

"What can I do for you?" the king asked.

"I don't need anything," the animal said. "It's I who've come to help you."

"No one can help me," the king said.

"What do you want?" the animal asked.

"I want the rain to fall and my kingdom to be happy as it was," the king said. "And for my heart not to be hard any more."

"Why do you want those things?" the animal asked.

"Can you doubt that I want them?" the king said.

"I see no reason to believe it."

"Do you think I'm indifferent to the state of the kingdom?" the king asked.

"No, I don't think that."

There was a pause. The king looked into the holes that were the animal's eyes.

"Where did you come from?" he asked.

"I used to live here," the animal answered. "Before this palace was built. Before anything was built here."

"I thought all the beasts from those days were dead," the king said.

"What do you know about death?" the animal answered.

"How do you propose to help?" the king asked.

"Here," said the animal, tearing a tuft of fur from its breast. "Take this. Give it to your elder son. Send him to the northern part of the plateau, to the driest place. Tell him to make a hole in the ground with his hands and plant this tuft of hair. When he has done that I will come back and tell you what you owe me."

The animal turned and went slowly across the throne room, with its claws clicking on the darkened stones, and out the door.

The king sat in the dark with the fur in his hand, turning it, fingering it. It was damp to the touch. It offered no explanations. He had to admit that he was afraid, and not sure why. What should he do now? He did not believe that the fur would make any difference to anything, but what if it did? What might it do? What might the animal demand in return? Though surely if he did nothing now it would seem as though he really were indifferent to the state of his kingdom. It would be a proof that his heart was growing still harder. He sat pondering the matter for the rest of the afternoon and only when night fell did he call his elder son.

The young man had too profound a respect for his father, for the throne, and for his father's unhappiness to show any surprise. He took the fur from his father's hand and left that night.

By the next night he was back, but the news had travelled ahead of him. No sooner had he planted the fur, he said, in the driest place in the northern plateau, than a spring of water welled up from the spot and spread swiftly into a wide basin, brimming over and flowing away across the plain. If it went on, the pastures would begin to inch back over the shrivelled wastes. The sun would be a blessing again. A week passed, two weeks, a month, and the water went on flowing. The king felt a deadly misgiving in his heart but he could not run it to earth. The throne room remained dark. He waited for the animal to return.

And when the month was up the animal reappeared.

It came in and sat before the throne.

"Have I helped you?" it asked.

"I am not sure," the king answered.

"Has the water not come back?"

"It has."

"Is the grass not growing?"

"It is."

"Was that not what you wanted?"

"It was."

But the king knew that his own heart was as hard as ever. And yet he was ashamed to mention the fact to the animal, when the water had already made such a difference to the lives of many of his subjects. He felt that that would be selfish. It would also be difficult to explain. What do animals know about the hardness of human hearts?

"What do I owe you?" the king asked.

"I wish to be restored to my ancient office," the animal said. "I wish to be appointed Warden of the Waters, with full authority over the use of all the waters in your kingdom."

The king bowed his head and thought. Had he the right, he asked himself, to grant to an animal control over the prosperity and even the lives of his subjects, to leave their welfare and their futures in the hands of a creature he knew nothing about except that water came from its planted fur? That was the first objection he admitted to himself. Then there was another. Suppose the animal did administer the waters fairly and even magnanimously. The king's heart would remain unchanged. And it was the hardness of the king's heart, he reminded himself, that had caused the drought. If the water flowed now from some other cause, his heart might never be able to change again. And for another thing, could any relief of the drought that came from outside be regarded as trustworthy, in the circumstances, or even real?

"Ask something else," the king said. "I cannot give you that."

"You do not know what you want," the animal said. "But maybe you will find it anyway." It turned and went out of the throne room.

The next morning the elder son was found dead in his bed. And in the afternoon news came that the spring in the northern plateau had dried up. The king sat in the throne room, numb and cold.

A month passed. The drought was unchanged. Once again the animal stood before the king.

"There's no point in your coming again," the king said.

"Do you think that if your heart were to break—" the animal began.

"What?" the king asked, trying to look into the animal's eyes.

"Water would flow from the cracks, and everything else would be whole again?"

"It might be," the king answered. "But my heart will not break."

"How do you know?" the animal asked.

"It should have broken by now."

"Do you still care about your kingdom at all?"

"Would I be here otherwise?"

The animal tore out another tuft of its fur and held it out to the king.

"Give this to your other son," it said. "Tell him to take it to all the dry stream beds in the kingdom and drop a hair in each. I will come back and tell you what you owe me."

Once more, after the animal had gone, the king sat in silence pondering the tuft of fur in his hand, feeling as though he were drifting out over an abyss. In the evening he summoned his other son and told him what to do.

Day after day the news came in from the kingdom

that the streams were flowing again, the lakes were filling, the old mill wheels were beginning to turn with a terrible screeching and shrieking after so long standing parched and split. There were even fish in the streams and ponds, as large as though they had been growing through the whole time of the drought. The other son came home happy, with messages of affection and presents from all parts of the kingdom, and his carriage full of pretty girls. The king was polite. But he trusted nothing. He grew, if anything, more withdrawn. Curtains were made for the throne room, because the light hurt his eyes. A month after the return of his son, the animal reappeared.

"Great king," it said. And then it sat down in front of the throne.

"Why do you call me that?" the king asked.

"Because of you the kingdom is happy again."

"I wish it were so," the king said.

"You can make it so," the animal said.

"I do not know how."

"Give me my ancient office. Appoint me Warden of the Waters of your kingdom."

Once again the king considered the matter. Yes, suppose it was true that the animal could make the springs rise and the streams flow as it willed. What other powers might it not have that could involve the country in greater miseries than any it had yet suffered, if the king were once to grant the creature a position of such authority. And if the original cause of the kingdom's disasters lay, in fact, in the king's own heart, would any change of the external circumstances be likely to last? Would it be something on which to base the future of the kingdom? Would it not simply remove all hope that the king's heart might ever change? It was true that this time the king was afraid of the animal. But could he allow his own fears, even for those near him, to influence him in his duty to the kingdom?

"I have no right to grant you that," the king said.

"You know nothing about rights," the animal said. "And you will never know anything about them. You can give me what I ask. Or you can refuse."

"I cannot give you what you ask."

"You can give me whatever you want to give me. That is what a king is," the animal answered.

"No," the king said at last, still hoping that one day his heart might undergo a change. And the animal went away. The next day the king's other son was found dead in his bed, and the news began to come in that the streams were shrinking and the ponds drying up. At the king's orders the whole country went into mourning. All the flames in the hearths were covered with ashes and gave off nothing but smoke. White bones were hung against the doors and windows and rattled in the wind. At the end of a month the animal entered the dark throne room again. The king stared at the creature with hatred and dread.

"Why have you come back?" he asked. "We have nothing to say to each other. Each of us must pursue his own nature."

"I've no quarrel with that," the animal said. "But I keep thinking that I can help you. That's part of my nature. It's never changed."

"I won't make you any promises," the king said. "I am not sure of anything any longer except one quality of my own heart."

"Its darkness?" the animal asked.

"Its hardness," the king said.

"Here," the animal said, tearing out a third tuft of fur and holding it out to the king. "I'll try once more. Take this everywhere in your kingdom. From every rock on which you lay a hair, a trickle of clear water will begin to flow. From every hillside on which you lay a piece of fur a stream will begin. Merely brush the village fountains with the ends of it and they will leap into the air. Keep the fur. It will last you as long as you need it. I will ask you nothing in return. Not now. Not in the future."

The king felt the fur in his hand. He looked at the animal sitting in front of him. He looked at the empty eyes. He imagined going out with the fur, the springs flowing, the joy in the land. He thought of how he would owe all of that to this animal. And then he thought of his own heart. Nothing would ever change it again. The flocks would fatten, the people grow rich and happy and bless him. It would all be due to this beast who was really the warden of the waters. And meanwhile his heart would remain as hard as ever, and no happiness would be real, and one day, promise or no promise, the beast might return and demand—anything—. He stopped there.

There was a way out. It was hard, but it was a solution. Or at least it was a decision. It came from that very hardness of his heart. He thought of his dead sons. He thought of the possible threat to the future of the kingdom. He clutched the fur in his left hand and with his right he drew his sword, as he leapt to his feet. With one stroke he severed the animal's head from its shoulders.

And the candle went out. And the windows fell in. And the throne collapsed. And the ceiling peeled away like shavings and rolled down the crumbling walls. And from the animal's neck the fountain began to flow. The fountain of Llorndy, on its way to the salt. But the king fell back on the stones and from his heart the first of the oaks raised two tender leaves.

Being Born Again

Some days—and on occasion it lasts much longer—
the oppression stirs, shifts (it may seem at first to
be no more than a change of position) and I feel the labor begin again. However I move or wherever I go I
cannot get outside of this travail, which in itself, of
course, is a delivery from a confinement. The heaven
and the earth of this predicament are nowhere that I can
see. My eyes take in only the immediate world that my
own body inhabits, and they try to persuade me that the
old world is the only one. Because it is the only one that
they have developed habits to comprehend.

Seeing, though, has nothing to do with the travail. It
seems, rather, as though nothing that I had beheld up
until that day were of use in the pressure and the searing
desolation that come upon me. I must exist in many forms
at a given time, after all, only one of which I think I am
used to and have adopted as a convention. And the pressure has come from some other existence of myself, un-
known to me or at least unnoticed, that has grown,
curled in itself, until it can no longer be contained and
is now undergoing a change in its very cosmos.

Can no longer be contained in what, it may well be

asked. And I ask it, and send out all my senses like an-
guished balloons trying to find—what, who? The matrix,
the life which is crushing me, through which and from
which I am being torn. And yet the quest is hopeless, and
I know it. These senses cannot enter into and look out
from the life of that other who is suffering now pains of
which my own are mere distant echoes. My senses cannot
place that other being, nor define it. They can only learn
of it by leaving it. Then the suffering will remain with
them. Like a root torn out. It will have become their
own. No longer simply an echo, but the first possession,
the first knowledge of the new "I."

No, the new mother—there is no way of envisaging
her form, her place, anything about her except her own
pain, of which this pressure, this vertigo, this anguish,
this dread, this ferocity, this hope, this tenderness, this
hunger and this thirst are, or at least may be analogies—
or growths, flowers, or echoes, as I have said. They are
all beyond my control and presumably they are beyond
hers. The only way that I will be able to learn more
about her is by advancing through her and away from
her, in the grip of this suffering which we share, which
is nothing more or less than my being torn from her. It
is not, once again, as though either of us had a choice. In
anything except our willingness.

It is all very well to know this with what I have come
to call my reason. I cannot remember it, and only memory would help me at this point, it seems to me, on my
way into the new days. And the new nights. And memories do come at moments with messages, though whether
to guide or to distract me I cannot tell. In the midst of a
spasm which I tell myself (with a laugh) that I may not
survive, I have a sudden clear and indubitable glimpse of
myself lying in my mother's arms at a bay window facing south over a catalpa tree, in the sunlight. She has no
age, and no one else exists, and what passes between us

is a tenderness into which everything else crowds, shuffling its feet, then holding its breath, then at peace.

At other moments I hear the horses. It is not something that I could be said to remember, I suppose, because it cannot have been sent to my brain by my own body. It cannot belong to the nights that are to come. Can it? Can it be said to belong to the old ones? Can it come from the mother herself? There in front of me is darkness—a strip of torn earth with a blacker line of bushes beyond it, and a blacker canal or slow stream beyond that. I am being held up at a gate. Held up high, by a tall female figure, a very tall female figure in dark clothes that reach to the ground. Her hair is tied in a small knot on top of her head and a white collar circles her neck— the only white object. I never see her face. I feel the pulsing of her hands around my chest. It is almost in time with the sound of the hoofbeats. They are approaching from one side, galloping, thudding toward us, black circles, louder and louder. Then a black shape with a rider on it streaks past and is gone on the other side. But almost at once another rider streams past in the opposite direction. A coldness on my head, like a dark hand, may be wind. The thudding of the horses recedes, grows fainter, then approaches again. Again the riders streak past, one after the other, in their opposite directions. Again and again. A tiny sun is trying to rise in my throat. I fix my eyes on the glassy black water beyond the track. What will come down that current? I see only the paper boat which I know to be sleep, disappearing behind some willows. It had had something to tell me. It is sorry.

The whole scene comes and goes. At last, in a silence of great weariness, with a blow that I will always be expecting to feel repeated, the sun leaps into my head. The first of the new colors, like the old red, flows sadly into everything. It is naked. And the rawness that is my new heart begins to beat.

In a Dark Square

H E WHO has lost the key to the ancient lies which everyone held in common is wandering at night, by himself, in an empty square surrounded by featureless doors, with no one to listen to how many telephone numbers he has memorized. For however far-flung and ineradicable their influence by now has become, it is there that the lies still live, in those tall dark houses with lights showing only above each of the front doors to illumine the numbers, which appear to be in a script he cannot understand, though it looks like the only one with which he can honestly claim to be familiar. Lie numbers, ha ha. All his life he thought he knew better and after all that he has said and studied and, as he put it, thought, it is inside those doors, and he knows it, that the whole of reason is lying, asleep, secure in the age of inventors and large families, dreaming placid dreams in which he never even figures as a possible future.

He remembers what he has heard of them, the great families. The Origins, for instance: to himself he admits that for years he has been able to recognize those individuals whom the stork brought, those who were found in cabbages, those who came in a black bag, those who rolled in over the doorsill wrapped in a dust devil, those who were given away on a street corner with a pound of tea. Without his acknowledging the fact, this had frequently been his only means of telling them apart. Frequently? How frequently, he asks himself, and for how long? Feeling the night turn cold at the approach of truth.

He wonders whether the doors are in fact locked. He wonders whether anyone inside would hear him. He wonders how he might appeal to any of them if they woke. He wonders whether the handle would be noisy. He knows that he would be able to find his way unlit through the hall, up the stairs, along the landing, to his own room. Maybe they would not wake at all. Maybe, on the other hand, they would only pretend that they were asleep as he crept past their door, left open a crack so that they would hear him when he came in. Maybe they never sleep but simply wait for him to come in, wait and wait, sad and bitter and too old to change. If anyone is going to change he knows it will have to be him.

"Have they ever asked themselves," he says, glancing around to see whether the police are about, "have they ever asked themselves whether they were true to anything?"

He wonders what will happen if it starts to be day. The little lights, then, will still burn over the doors. They will grow yellow and fade as a new day brightens the lie numbers and he sees (for the first time, as he says) that each of the doors is crossed with colored ribbons, like a gift-wrapped package, complete with a huge bow and flowers. Then what? Are they really, all of them, presents sent from the old relatives whom he has never seen, the aunties, the grannies, the eyeless, the toothless, who have never seen him and yet presume to say what his whole life is to be? Will he finally (for the cold of the morning is terribly penetrating, after a night with no sleep, in the open) walk up the few steps, feeling a monument toppling inside him, and set his hand deliberately to the end of one of the ribbons, and undo the bow in the full knowledge that whatever that package contains will be his for the rest of his life?

"No," he says, thinking of the day warming up sooner or later and everything starting to resume just where it left off. "No," he says, "we have nothing to do with each other."

And though no one is listening he repeats aloud to the darkness that he will continue to put all his faith in himself.

Hope for Her

I N THE beginning hope for her was a large white cloth thickly covered with embroidery, also in white, so rich that it made the cloth curl like a board and so delicate that the sight of it would make you gasp, and she was not yet allowed even to touch it. She did not know what it was for. That would come some day. She certainly was not old enough to think of using it. It would be a long time before that. And beautiful though it was she seldom thought of it and was content to wait.

Still early, hope for her was a white backcloth like the sheet her mother hung against the wall for her to dance in front of when there was company, only much bigger, so that it stretched as high as any building and ran for a full block in either direction, and was smooth as the marble forehead of Diana. And in front of it how she would dance! They would hardly be able to believe it was she. And yet, yes it was! It was, it really was she! She would start using it soon. In a year or two.

Before long, hope for her was a pale moonish expanse, a shade of white, but one that had been brushed with age and had learned of the existence of parchment and bone, and of questions that she could not make out but remembered hearing, whispered, when they thought she was asleep. It was bare and troubling like the head of a drum, and there was a light behind it that would not remain still. But she did not need it yet.

One day when she actually wanted the drum, that very drum, to lay her ear against—something that would be cool and not go away as many things she had known better had been doing—it broke not a foot from her head. Inside she saw that it was dark, empty, very old. It remembered someone else whom she had never known. A few tiny scraps of tan newspaper were stuck in the rim here and there. The innards of a light bulb were swinging back and forth on the end of a string. She seized the torn edges of the stiff calf-skin and tried to pull them back together again, crying (she told herself) "as she had never cried before." But all that that meant was that she had begun a new kind of forgetting.

For a long time after that hope for her was a calm lake in early spring, white because the sky above it was the color of milk. She knew that the lake was hers. She knew that it would remain hers as long as she never went there. It remained hers for a long time. She scarcely dared look at it very often. Just from time to time, out of the corner of her eye. She did not want to seem to be spying. Besides, she was afraid of water. Bushes grew up between her and the lake. In time she could scarcely see it at all. Sometimes, with a catch in her breath, she suddenly thought that it might have been taken away. But then she would laugh. How could anyone remove a lake? Was it really hers, though, she wondered. Could she be sure? But she told herself to be sensible. If she stopped and breathed quietly she could feel that it was still there.

At last hope for her was a glass jar in which she was standing. The air was cool. The glass was a little blue, like ice, but perfectly clear. She had room to move a little. She was not cold. Outside the jar a first snow was falling: huge soft flakes of white paper. As they came near the jar they whirled around it and some of them stuck to it, lower down, and clung. They had covered the whole of the outside of the jar with a coat of white feathers, up as far as her neck. From outside, she realized, she looked beautiful. She must never have looked so beautiful. The whole lower part of the jar was like lighted alabaster, and above the line of the feathers her head appeared inside the glass, the skin smooth and radiant, the eyes calm, clear and bright. But she knew that now it was her face inside the jar that was attracting the snow which had gradually blotted out her body. The flakes circled the jar in front of her face like white bees going home. They lit on the glass whenever she breathed. She tried not to breathe. She tried to keep one spot clear. Little by little, flake by flake, the whiteness covered everything except one small area through which one of her eyes could be seen, large and clear and beautiful. Then that too was covered and whiteness was all she had.

The Medal of Disapproval

It has, of course, two sides.

There is the side without a face. On this side the symbols are arranged like objects in the nest of a rat—fixed, neatly interrelated, but so far from their original backgrounds and purposes that it is often hard to say what they are. On the other hand it is obvious that they bespeak immeasurable age, and an authority that is on intimate terms with the order of the cosmos itself. Indeed they may be interpreted as being an extension of that order. Sometimes there is a laurel crown. Empty. Occasionally there is a lamp. Often, in fact almost always, there are numbers. This side is clearly abstract and there is no appeal to it. It is the side that is presented, in due course, to the person disapproved of.

Then there is the other side called the face. And in fact it has a head on it. The head of a ruler, a hero of some kind, a forbear. But whatever motto surrounds him, his face is turned away. It is turned away forever. There is no appeal to this side, either. It too is abstract. This is the side that is worn facing outward, by the disapproving. Then the other side is worn facing inward.

Forgetting

FIRST you must know that the whole of the physical world floats in each of the senses at the same time. Each of them reveals to us a different aspect of the kingdom of change. But none of them reveals the unnameable stillness that unites them. At the heart of change it lies unseeing, unhearing, unfeeling, unchanging, holding within itself the beginning and the end. It is ours. It is our only possession. Yet we cannot take it into our hands, which change, nor see it with our eyes, which change, nor hear it nor taste it nor smell it. None of the senses can come to it. Except backwards.

Any more than they can come to each other.

Yet they point the way. And most authoritatively as they disappear. Was that their office, after all? Was their disappearance what they were?

At the top of a ladder each rung of which disappears as we climb, there is a little window that looks across a narrow strip of ground covered in thin grass yellowed by summer and twitching with wind in the cool light of late afternoon. The window is sealed. There is no sign of a path through the grass. Across the strip of ground there is a white wall too high for us to be able to see the top of it. Someone is pressed against it looking through a little window.

In which one can make out a narrow strip of ground covered with round pebbles spotted dark green over which water and bits of green-brown weed wash, cling, spread, hide. Instead of sea, at the other side of the strip of shore there is a granite wall with a small window in it and someone there looking through.

In the window can be seen a narrow strip of green hills with sheep and the shadows of clouds moving over them and beyond them a gray stone wall with a little window in it and someone gazing through. Into a narrow strip of night with tree branches hanging low over a river, and beyond that the foot of a wall.

Somewhere on the other side of that a voice is coming. We are the voice. But we are each of those others. Yet the voice is coming to us. That is what we are doing here. It has to pass through us. It has to pass through us in order to reach us. It has to go through us without pausing in order to be clear to us. Only in the senses can we pause because only in the senses can we move. The stillness is not in the senses but through them and the voice must come through the stillness. Each in turn we must become transparent. The voice will not change but we will. Will it reach us before we are unrecognizable? Will we be able to receive it? Will we not be in our way?

We close our eyes. Darkness unrolls over the strips of ground and the walls, over everything except the windows, and the heads gazing through them.

We listen to the sounds from the strips of ground. More strips than we could see. Each of them hears the voice, each of them repeats rumors of it but all we hear is the repetition, not the voice. One by one we come to the end of each of these sounds and replace it with a silence of the same size. The silence is not the voice but it carries echoes of it. One by one we come to the ends of the echoes.

One by one the tastes come. They have all been living in the past. They bow and pass on with their trays empty or piled with artificial fruit, and without expression, as though we were nothing to them.

The textures come, the sensations, unwinding themselves from the other senses, from time, from the darkness on which they grew, from the fear that is their mother. They fade. Now nothing can be felt in the darkness.

The odors come, the stepping-stones in the air, the clothes floating in nothing, reminding of the limbs that had worn them into endless ages. Tears pour down. The clothes dissolve.

There is still memory itself. The back of the head. The backs of the heads blocking the windows. One by one we forget them and the walls are forgotten.

Fire has gone. It is cool at last. There is no light.

Earth has gone. We float in a small boat that was once green, at an immense height on the unlit sea. No, there is no height, for the depth of the water is infinite. Good-bye height, good-bye depth. The sea is everywhere. It has no shores. Above us the air of this sea. The black space. The stars have all moved out of sight. The night extends beyond them into emptiness.

Then the water has gone and there is only the small boat floating in nothing in the dark. With it the directions have gone. There is only the boat floating in nothing, in the dark, without directions, without size. You cannot feel it. You cannot smell it. You cannot taste it. Then it has gone.

Then nothing has gone.

The voice must have come. Because it has gone.

Mariette

W HEN you go, go up the road slowly until you
first see the lake on your right. Be careful not to
miss the first lane that turns off toward the water, almost
as soon as the water comes into sight through the trees.
You might go right past because the lane is small and has
grass growing in the middle. And no mailboxes, and
bushes on both sides of it.

It leads off at a slight angle and the bushes don't last
for long. You look back and see that the road isn't in
sight any more, and then you look ahead and see that
you are coming out into open country. A pasture slopes
down from the left, smoothed, and continuing beyond
where you can see, catching the light. Sometimes cows,
sometimes sheep, sometimes horses, sometimes nothing.
You breathe the breath of pastures. You remember that
the lake is very high. There are no fences, and the grazed
slope, without a bush or a tree on it, continues its descent
on the other side of the lane, all the way to the water
where it ends here and there in ferns or reeds, or runs
straight into the lake without anything. It's hard to tell
how far away the shore is. The lane leads ahead—a
narrow level groove on the green slope, in the gray light.

At some distance, where the lane draws near to the edge of the lake, you see a building set facing the water. One end of it, the end nearer to you, appears to be a house. A little porch in front, a little porch in back, white boards, green trim. The other end, which is bigger but not so high, you can see is the store. The windows are broader and things are piled there with darkness waiting behind them. Sheets of tin with people's heads on them smiling, and names of tobaccos in the old colors, and signatures of forgotten soft drinks, are nailed to the unpainted façade. In front of the store a long boat dock runs out over the lake, very uneven, low to the water, with fishing poles stuck on it at the end, fishing.

You feel your stomach contract at the nearness of the lake.

Marietta will be coming down the lane. Almost certainly. You'll see why when you meet her. You can't imagine Marietta ever having been late for anything. When you catch sight of her she'll probably be at least two thirds of the way from the store to where you are standing as you turn back to look ahead after your first pause to take in the whole slope running down to the lake. You will see the heavy but graceful figure, in the long dark skirt, swinging toward you, and it is only a moment before you will be standing face to face. Marietta never wears a hat. Most people who never wear hats look natural without them. Marietta usually looks as though she had just taken hers off and her head was enjoying an unaccustomed nakedness about which nothing will be said. Something of the same quality emanates from Marietta herself and immediately includes you. Her loose stride brings her up to you quickly and she stops as though she could not pause. When she talks the voice seems to come from the whole of her body. Anyone can always hear what she has to say.

And you stand there together above the lake while she

tells you about how you look, which isn't bad. You can see that she's been through it. You can tell that from her face, young though it still looks, and lighting up as she talks, like a girl's. But when she laughs her calm laugh you can see that it's not in ignorance. Of anything.

Then if it's an even day she leads you back on your tracks a little way to a path worn through the pasture, running down toward the lake, but away from the store, into the woods. She talks about winters as though they were immense white visitors whom you have never met but who know about you. She talks about the spring, the fish, the coming of the summer. All the time you are in the woods full of pipestems and ferns and marshy patches that you cross on hummocks of grass, and she swings along in her torn jacket and finally falls silent, and a minute later leads you out into the little clearing by the backwater.

The place is utterly still. On the left, where you've come from, the woods are lush and green. The path goes on to the right through more woods, around the edge of the water, where it's almost dark. And in front of you there are more trees, looking as though they grew out of a black stretch of the water itself, which is connected with the lake and the light only by a narrow inlet. In the shadowy backwater a small white flat-bottomed boat will be floating. And in it a girl in a white dress, reading a book.

That's Flora. You know, she's older than you. You feel a ringing in your collar-bones and Marietta reaches down to a rope tied to a tree and pulls the boat ashore, and then smiles at you and leaves you with Flora.

You remember Flora but you're shy and don't want her to know that you are. But she doesn't seem to notice. What a nice girl. You go out in the boat for a little while. You don't need to row anywhere, but you do, a little bit. The woods turn. You can see the undersides of her thighs as she sits looking around. What a nice girl. And she likes you. You can tell quite soon that she likes you a lot. She talks to you about books, and she tells you that she likes talking to you about books, and you hear a beating in your throat and over your eyes like somebody running, and your mouth is dry and the corners are stiff. You can hardly swallow and you can't answer her without swallowing, and she keeps looking at you and smiling and doesn't seem to notice. They say she's very intelligent. And so quiet. And well-mannered. She leans forward with her elbows on her knees and you can look down inside the opening of the front of her dress into the dark cleft between her breasts and almost to the end of one full perfect pointed breast. You never know what it will look like until you see it. She sees that you're looking. She smiles, and she doesn't move at all, except a little bit from side to side. She waits for you to look up. You do. She goes on smiling. She leans farther forward and pushes your hands on the oars and you both row back to the clearing in silence.

You fumble, tying up the boat, while she waits in the back. She's a nice girl. You keep swallowing. You hear everything through glass. You step out and hold out your hand to her and she gets up and steps over the seats and onto the ground. You put your hand around her waist, just seeing if you can, but she lets you. Then she puts her arm around you and starts walking along the path into the woods. She's quite a lot older.

You come to where she's left her things, in a grassy place under the trees. A basket. More books. A blanket. You stare for a minute not knowing what you can do next and hoping that she hasn't by now forgotten that minute in the boat, or decided to pretend to forget it or that it was just your imagination and you really should be ashamed. You hear how small your voice is as you say "Let's sit down."

She sits down and you see more of her legs. She doesn't seem to be trying to hide them. You look down her dress again, partly to make sure you can, and she catches your eyes again and smiles. You sit down beside her and put your arm back around her waist and she leans against you. You're shivering. You just sit there, wondering if you can kiss her, staring at nothing. Then you try. You have to turn her shoulders around, and it's awkward and doesn't work very well, but then she lies down full length on the blanket, with one knee a little in the air and the skirt far up her thigh, and you put both arms around each other and she starts teaching you what to do with your mouth. Very patient. And then she presses her body against you all the way down and that's something you've thought about a lot and you try it too.

When she lies back from you she throws an arm up onto the grass above her head so that the dress is stretched tight over her breast, and then after a minute she pushes off her shoes and raises her head to look down at her feet and then looks at you. The top two buttons of her dress are already unbuttoned. It's that kind of dress. Her hand drops to the next one and stays there but you still can't be quite sure that she's not pretending or that you're not mistaken and so you still don't dare put your hand on her breast, not even as though you weren't aware of what you were doing so that she can pretend she doesn't notice it. She undoes the button herself.

And then you undo a button at her waist and slide your hand in where it's warm and feels as though it were shining. You know your hand is cold, and you're shivering harder. You kiss again, and start to undo each others' clothes while you're kissing, and only stop when you have to, so that she can slip out of her dress and her bra while you watch, taking off your shirt and your shoes and pants. You look at her, and then, looking straight at you, she slowly pulls off her underpants and you pull off yours, with your throat almost closed up, and you let your eyes rest on the mound of brown hair and then lie down beside her and from there on start to act as though you knew what to do with everything. And she knows.

That's if it's an even day.

If it's an odd day Marietta asks you everything about your trip and about the winter, making it sound like a dark unpleasant building that's been bad for your health, and all the time she's leading you along toward the house and the store.

The store smells of ponds, fishing tackle, dogs, mothballs, and wet leather. She gives you some coffee at a table in the back and hangs up your things, talking all the time like a very old friend. She puts on some dance music a little out of date. She sits watching you eat a piece of cake, with coffee. She knows you don't drink coffee. She leads you into the back. The big room for dances and weddings. There's a pin-ball machine; they just got it. Nobody else is around. You've got a lot of nickels. She says she's got some more. She leaves you to it, with the music. You can stay there all day. And there are magazines. And at the far end of the room there's a door one step up that opens into some stairs, at the top of which is the bedroom of a girl named Flora who's a lot older than you and reads all the time and said she'd teach you to play cards. She's very pretty but she's a very nice girl, everybody says. She's probably up there reading all the time that you're at the pin-ball machine. Probably nobody else is coming, all afternoon. You could probably go up and see if she really would teach you to play cards. If she remembers. The music goes on and on. Your chest thumps as you walk across to the door and look up the stairs. And besides if anybody came by and asked what you were doing inside on a day like this, Marietta can be counted on to tell them never mind.

Graphology

I KNOW nothing about it, I realize. Whose fault is that? Do I understand anything of its principles? Does it proceed on the assumption or presupposition at least that every act we make reveals everything we are, if we could learn to read it? Do I believe that? Or simply that there is nothing that we can do that is not ourselves? Is that the same thing? Do I believe that? Who is ourselves? Does ourself do anything at all? Does it hold a pencil? Is not holding a pencil already a peculiarity? Is it only peculiarities that we reveal? Is it only peculiarities that we know how to read? Is that what we are?

In the lines we make on paper to signify something else to us, the will is always involved. But how, and to what extent? Does this study ask those questions? Not the will at the moment of writing alone, but its history, perhaps, its relation to the subject of the writing, and the history of its relation to that. Does the study consider these matters relevant? Can it in the end isolate the will from what appear to be the manifestations of the will? Is such an isolation possible? If it is can this study trace the difference between the will and the will's performance as that difference changes at every moment along the course of an intricate looping line meaning something else to the person who made it—a process which he learned with great expenditure of effort and time, some years before? Yes, learned with great invocation of care over a number of years, during which he was persuaded and long believed that excellence consisted of the absence of peculiarity in producing a line that was as near as possible to being no one's.

Is this study an art? Is it a science? Which would be better at present? Is it simply a crabbed face over one's shoulder saying that it's there to help one? Spotting peculiarities? Insisting that one begin again?

As if one could. Does it take that into consideration? There is no going back over that line's loops and breaks and abrupt changes of direction. They will have to read it from what is there. Some point that is there and will never be reached again. Altogether there are not more than a few miles to any such line, and then no more. The line that tries to go back is itself going forward.

But suppose this study possesses, in fact, the often unpleasant powers of uninvited helpers. Will it not, as they frequently do, know too much from the beginning, and use its knowledge to learn more things that one does not want it to know? Will it not be able to look at a few inches of line that I have put on a page in the sequence of what I learned once to consider my mistakes, and descry all the hidden weaknesses, secret inconsistencies, carefully concealed dead patches, dishonesties, cruelties, and beneath that, and beneath that? Will it say "He stopped here because he was weak"? Will it stop there? Why have I hidden those things? Will it disclose that?

Will it be able to take a segment of curved line and announce what exact place in the author's person produced that curve? And why? Will it become possible and desirable to consider the lines on their own, apart from their authors and their authors' wills, to think of them as having lives of their own to examine, to pick them up off the paper and hold them in your hands and listen to them breathing? Will the practise of this study become like counting? Or will it be—is it now, sometimes—like running along a path made in the snow by someone else, trying to glimpse that other while he remains just too far ahead among the trees, trying to understand his nature by tracing the strange curves of his single path? Then will your own path follow after you along the other person's? Will it be anxious to keep up with you? Will it sometimes fail? Will you ever turn and see that your own path has lost you? Will it find you at last, with all its secrets that you need? Will it lead you back? Will your own line and the line you are following become tangled? Will you look ahead to see whether their getting tangled doesn't make the other person look back? Will it? Will yours lead you back? Will you come to understand the line you are following so completely that you will be able to project it on ahead to somewhere the other person has not yet taken it, and call to him, "Be careful! Stop! Don't go on, that's out over nothing!" But be too late even so, for the line runs its course. Do I believe that? And the self—does it follow? Where? Was it the peculiarity all the time, that you could deduce but not know, trace but not alter, call out to but not save?

Will something lead you back?

Phoebe

SHE USED to sit at a window of a big house and imagine herself when she was grown up. How beautiful
she would be. And how kind. There she stood, looking
down at Phoebe the child. She held out her hand to
touch the child but the hand turned to air. Often she
would tell Phoebe something. Oh, there was little she
would not have told Phoebe, in time. How beautiful her
voice was. But when the child looked at her and watched
the lips moving she heard nothing. It was only later that
she remembered the words, and the sound.

Phoebe tried to draw her picture but it was never like
her. She tried to talk in her voice but it never sounded
like her. She tried to repeat her words but when she did
that she forgot them.

One day when Phoebe was sitting at the window
imagining herself when she grew up, she saw that she
was standing there more beautiful than ever, in gorgeous
clothes, but in tears. She was trying to tell the child
something. Phoebe had never tried so hard to listen, but
she heard nothing. She began to cry too, but she tried
not to so that she could look and listen. It was only later,
when she was alone again, that she remembered the
words.

They said that now that she was grown up she was
going away. Someone important was coming to fetch
her. That was why she was wearing those beautiful
clothes. He was going to take her to his own house a
long way from there. She would never come back.
When she remembered the words Phoebe was too
frightened to cry. Not only because she was afraid of
whoever was coming. Not only because she never
wanted to go away. Not only because she tried to repeat
the name of the person who was coming, and of the
place where he was going to take her, as she remembered
them, and so had forgotten them.

She was frightened because all at once she no longer
wanted to grow up, because there would be nobody
there. After a while she ran down into the woods and
began calling, "Phoebe, Phoebe," softly. You can hear
her, but she has never been found.

PHOEBE lived beside woods. She was very shy. She had
reached the age when her parents had begun to talk
about her getting married. But all she wanted to do was
to spend her time with the birds, listening to them. All
the birds knew her and would sing when she was there.
She had discovered that if she really listened, each of
their voices made something happen to her. When the
sparrow cheeped she could feel her blood moving. When
the swallows chattered she could remember things from
her infancy that she had forgotten. When the crow
cawed she could see the darkness in everything. There
was one gray bird who was silent. She used to believe
that if that bird called her name she would vanish.

One night in the house her parents were talking about
her. They thought she was asleep. How old they looked,
she thought. No bird she knew was ever so old. Her
hands were cold. Her lips were cold. She heard nothing,
except her own name coming from one or the other, in

an undertone. She fell asleep. She dreamed of what their voices did to her. They took her by the hands and led her out into a place without trees. On and on they walked, the three of them, in the dark. There was not a sound. Her hands hurt. They hurt worse and worse. But when she pulled on them pieces of them came off. Her parents held her by the blood and walked on. She tried to say something to them, she tried to scream something to them, but she found that she had no voice. She looked at them and saw that their lips were moving but she heard nothing. She saw that they were getting older and older as she watched, and a grief, a fear, a coldness such as no bird voice had ever made her feel gripped her throat and her stomach so that she thought she would die of it. And they were taking her with them. Yet she did not want them to go on alone, without her, and grow older and older, while she was there alone with only pieces of her hands, bleeding. She woke. Her face was wet with tears. Day was breaking. The dream was still with her. It would not leave her. She jumped out of bed and ran to the door. The dream went with her. She flung the door open and ran into the woods. From a window of the house her mother leaned out to call after her as she disappeared.

Then suddenly the gray bird started calling, "Phoebe."

WHEN Phoebe and the young ruler had been married a year their union was blessed with a daughter. The people would have preferred a son. The young ruler would have preferred a son. But Phoebe was happy with the little girl, who was very beautiful and sweet-natured.

The people and the young ruler were prepared to wait. But year after year passed and Phoebe and the young ruler had no more children. At the end of seven years the young man consulted his mother about what to do to have a son. She said, "Either your wife must go, and you must get another. Or else the little girl must go." The young man did not want to send his wife away so he decided that it would have to be the little girl.

"What do you mean 'she must go' "? he asked.

"She must not remain in this world," his mother said.

That same night he called in a man he could trust and told him to seize the child as she slept, cover her mouth with a sleeve, cover her eyes with a sleeve, tie her arms, and lead her far out into the forest where the animals would eat her.

And it all happened.

And in the morning Phoebe came into the child's room and found the bed empty. On the floor beside it were a few gray feathers. There were more by the door. And on the stairs. And on the stones outside. And on the road. She began to run. All the way along the road there were those same feathers. The road led into the woods. She began to call. The name of the child was Phoebe.

The Trembler

WHEN I thought about Mr. Jameson it was, I am afraid, usually because his own situation so closely paralleled mine. We have both been working for years—for decades, to be honest—in the same building, he on the nineteenth and I on the twenty-third floor. And whatever titles our firms have given to our respective positions to dignify them in accordance with our advancing years, both of us, to designate it by its correct name, are (let me say) little other than office boys. Clearly by now we will never be anything more. On the other hand we are secure in our unchallenging positions. Both of us are employed by large, well-established, sober firms that would obviously survive any reverse short of a total collapse of the national economy. And within these firms we are taken for granted. We are among the oldest employees. Each of us has been serving his respective firm longer than the firm's president himself. In the event of a setback, even an important one, you may be sure that many younger and breezier men who are our superiors, even to some little distance up the scale, would be given notice long before we would be informed that our services were no longer required. In fact that latter contingency is virtually unimaginable. One turns to it sometimes, alone in the elevator, as something which will afford a passing sigh of relief on an otherwise uneventful day.

Over the years our calling has thrown us together not closely, you might say, but frequently, and we have come to know each other as fixtures of each other's days. Familiars, if I might put it that way, without being intimates. To be honest, the sight of Mr. Jameson troubled me slightly for years, in a fashion that at one time I would not perhaps have admitted. But advancing age has brought a certain reckless candor to my mental processes, something which, let me add, supplies a touch of exhilaration, on occasion, to my thoughts, and I now recognize without the least trouble that the consideration of Mr. Jameson is sometimes unpleasant to me simply because it is hard for me to avoid altogether seeing in him a mirror of my own circumstance and even my own gestures and person. I contend against any such identification, I limit it severely, in fact, with my reason, but who at my age can honestly entertain many illusions about the power of that desperate and over-extended faculty, I sometimes ask, considering the abyss into which we are all happily travelling.

It is within the framework of this situation that my curiosity about one aspect of Mr. Jameson's behavior, as it struck me at least, is to be viewed. I confess that it led me to indulge in a closeness of scrutiny which I now see that I disguised from myself for some time, verging, as it did, on the critical.

I cannot remember what particular detail occasioned it, but I well recall the excitement that imbued the entire day when once I admitted to myself that there seemed to me to be something about Mr. Jameson that I could only call furtive. I could give my mind to little else: the quality itself, and then of course whatever might be its real or imaginary source. Were either of these known and recognized by Mr. Jameson himself? I paid more attention to him, needless to say, from then on. In fact I watched him so closely that I was soon at some pains to conceal the eagerness of my observation. I am afraid that I undertook, more and more boldly, the role of sympathizer. My very eyes, if we found ourselves alone on the elevator together, came to infer, as nearly as I could manage it, that to know all is to forgive all, with the further implication that there was little in this mortal world that was strange to me. Whether or not my success can be laid at the door of this countenance which became, in due course, habitual with me in my meetings with Mr. Jameson, the fact is that something, and very possibly something about me, awoke in him a feeling of confidence where I was concerned. The suspicious but helpless confidence of a younger brother, perhaps, who knows that his candor will be abused, but who is irresistibly drawn, even so, to lay bare his paltry secrets one by one, grubbing down and down for deeper and perhaps more interesting ones. Gradually Mr. Jameson took to smiling at me in a peculiar draggled way like an ugly girl's from under an umbrella, and I knew that I was, as they say, making progress.

What vice could he have, I wondered, that had wrapped him to itself so tightly and so completely that his judgment had remained stunted by it—the faculty of a boy in pimples. With what vice of his had he not come to terms—or sufficiently so as to be able to brazen it out, at least—by his age? The matter seemed, to be honest, to present opportunities, and I watched, with an excitement which I will not venture to describe, the development of his smile on the occasions that permitted it. And fully prepared for it though I was—or so I imagined—it was with a marked quickening of the pulse and dryness of the mouth that I welcomed his first sudden painfully awkward lurch toward confidences.

In all the years that we had worked together and had gone down the elevator together in the evenings on our separate ways to our lodgings we had never—even when, as sometimes happened, we were leaving late at the same time—so much as invited each other to share a coffe or a drink before our leisure hours rolled open in front of us. That particular evening the elevator was crowded. Mr. Jameson gave me only a glance as he got on, and in it no sign of recognition. As though simply to make sure that I was there. All the way down his eyes remained fixed on the gray overcoat on the back of the man standing in front of him. He got off ahead of me. I was outside the main door when I found him beside me, asking me under his breath whether I wouldn't like a drink on my way home.

Of course I did what I could to make him feel at ease with regard to the disclosures upon which he had decided to embark. As might have been expected, several drinks were necessary, and at least an hour of faltering luckless talk. Then slowly it became apparent that Mr. Jameson's furtiveness was in fact the obverse, as I had suspected, of a secret arrogance stemming from a practice of which he was the sole devotee. He confessed it at last: his private inexhaustible pleasure, the exigeant delight which he himself had invented. It was trembling.

It was exclusively a private activity, he explained. By now he was sure that it would be impossible for him to tremble in any public situation, though he had fantasies of doing so which frightened him into a peculiarly exquisite form of indulgence in his secret practice. He described a few of the fears that he had drawn on in the early days of his vice—before, as he put it, he knew what he was about. Rather commonplace fears of parents, of teachers, of other boys, or girls. He described the dawning of his awareness that his vice was in itself a protection against such fears. It allowed him to welcome them as potential sources of pleasure. Of what he insisted was the subtlest and most luxurious of sensual and imaginary satisfactions. He tried to distinguish, for my benefit, as he said, the principle forms of the pleasure itself, dividing them in a manner that was evidently clearer to him than it was to me, into physical and spiritual delights, but he confessed with a disarming frankness that the separation often seemed arbitrary and meaningless. The one question about his practice which he could not fathom at all was why no one else appeared to have discovered it. He was forced to wonder what was lacking in everyone else. Or did many others keep it secret?

He described for me the manner in which trembling, properly conceived, became what could only be called an activity of the soul, whereby every possible source of dread was imaginatively conjured from the circumstances of a given life and then taught to perform its peculiar dance in which the entire emotional being of the participant was caught up, sometimes to the point of ecstasy, of self-annihilation. Did I not see that the practice did away with the old separation of inner and outer, subjective and objective, self and environment, in one profound vibrancy? Did I not see, did I not see? The fervor was all in his voice. I looked at his face, his mouth. They were impassive. His hand on his glass was as motionless as the table.

Could I not conceive, he asked, even without any but (he requested my forgiveness) the most ordinary and natural experience of the subject, and (he took the liberty of assuming) the most conventional of attitudes toward it, could I not conceive of the joy of finding oneself alone with a new, an unexplored source of fear or mortification or uncertainty—and the more imaginary the better? They were kept as it were in the middle foreground or the near background for a while—an artful pretense of putting them out of one's mind while at the same time enjoying their presence as they grew to what appeared to be autonomous strength and at last seemed to thrust themselves upon one, eclipsing everything else. Then one could allow the trembling to begin. He described the main external forms, the trembling of the hands, of the legs, of the stomach, of the muscles of the chest, of the insides of the upper arms, of the insides of the thighs, of the viscera, of the genitalia, and the sensations that each might be said, very roughly, to produce. He described the purely artificial focussing of the activity in the eyelids, in one eyelid, in one cheek, in one finger. He told of the silence that at last entered the exhausted limb—a calm that in his view must prefigure that of the dead, when their crude shakings have ceased at last.

For it was exhausting, he admitted. And from there he went on to discourse upon the privations which his pleasures forced upon him. How could he, he asked me, spare himself any dread or anguish or prospect of uncertainty, any sleeplessness or deliberate deprivation, in the indulgence of so vast, so heavenly (it was his own word) a delight? Sometimes, he told me, he feared for his health. But he laughed as he said it.

I looked closely at my own discomfort.

But what were these privations, he went on, when each of them in turn, as he now realized, was a promise of new bliss. He had the great good fortune, he confessed, to be of a profoundly timid temperament. The very furtiveness which had been his from early youth, and which he had carefully nurtured over the years in dealing with the rest of the world until now he might almost say with some small pride that it was perhaps the distinguishing trait of his personality (he looked to me for confirmation of this statement and I am afraid I nodded) had become in itself at once an outward sign of his adherence to his secret practice and a ceaseless contribution to it.

Could I imagine, he asked me, what it meant to him to be able to confide in someone?

We drank for a moment in silence.

He told me then that he considered himself an extremely happy man. We raised our glasses.

The Animal Who Eats Numbers

ONE IS just one. The animal eats it but apparently he makes no difference to it. Nothing does.

Two is a little girl in a starched muslin dress and patent leather shoes. She has on a red cardigan with a flower machine-embroidered on a pocket in front. Her thick dark hair is in bangs over her forehead and hangs almost to her shoulders on the sides and in back. She is good. She is never dirty. Everybody likes her. She is quiet. She always seems to be waiting and almost always smiling. Sometimes you look around—she has been pulling up her sock or something of the kind—and she has disappeared and everybody fusses and starts looking for her, but realizing of course that it couldn't be her fault. Usually it's because he has eaten her. For a little while. But it's such a nice day. Maybe her mother will let her come out again later, for a little while.

Three is a bigger boy without much to say for himself. He's big for his age and his clothes are too big for him and he has weak eyes. He's off by himself a lot but he doesn't get eaten very often. Sometimes he calls "Watch out!"—but usually he's not the one the animal wants. He's alright, though.

Four is eaten a lot. Very often she looks as though it's dark beyond her. You can hardly see her. Even when she's out she must be thinking.

Five is overweight. He laughs. The teacher doesn't like him much but he's funny and kind. He gets eaten all the time. He says he doesn't care. His clothes are all old anyway. He says he'd rather get eaten than do homework any day. He says he sits and plays cards with the animal as though he were at the firehouse.

Six is two's older sister. She wears yellow, mostly. She's good too. She hates being eaten. It doesn't happen to her very often. She thinks about going to college all the time. She thinks you don't get eaten there. Everybody respects her. She's terribly clean. When she gets eaten sometimes nobody notices, but if they do they're just quiet for a minute because they don't know what to say, and then they forget.

Seven is a quiet man in old clothes, including an overcoat and a hat. The teacher doesn't like him much but she never refers to him any more than necessary. He's often on the other side of the street and stops to look before he goes on to wherever he's going. Sometimes he has a satchel. He doesn't do any harm, but people don't like him. The animal doesn't like him either, and would only eat him if he were very hungry.

Eight is a cheerful nice lady in a flowered dress who seems to know everybody though nobody's quite sure who she is. The teacher doesn't mind what you're doing if she's around. Most of the time she doesn't seem to understand what anybody says, though. She's pretty fat. She gets eaten quite often too, but both she and the teacher like to pretend it doesn't happen. And to tell the truth nobody has ever actually seen her get eaten. It's just known.

Nine is another lady, a friend of the teacher's, thinner, with glasses, and very stern. She wears a dark red felt hat and an overcoat and carries a black patent leather pocket book. She resents very much the fact that she gets eaten sometimes. She probably fights with her elbows, but that wouldn't matter to the animal. She acts as though her being eaten were three's fault, five's fault, or seven's fault, whichever of them is handy. Three and five pretend to think she's a joke, but they don't really. Seven doesn't say anything and some people think he secretly likes her. Sometimes she's eaten for days at a time.

Ten is a very rich couple who never come near. If they go out it must be in their car. Apparently they get eaten too, though. The teacher and eight have been heard talking about it out in the hall. It was plain that they didn't really care.

The animal doesn't eat anything else, that we know of. The numbers know all about him and they don't worry. He never eats them for long and almost never if they're doing something. Besides, there are just as many of them as there ever were, and everyone says the future is theirs. It's the animal who is disappearing.

New Arrival

YES, this is the right train. Or it looks like it. The dirt is familiar. The smell. The advertisements. The rattle. Yes, the air—the same. And the same featureless country, brushing the windows hopelessly with its leaves curled and papery at the edges from bruises got by tapping the train again and again, trying to say heaven knows what. I sometimes think he's calling off stations I don't know, that they've got onto another line, I took the one on the wrong side of the platform. No. I'm going home.

There's the little river. Hasn't changed. It always looks a little different. They put something different beside it, that's it. They move the houses a few feet one way or the other. They have dogs drinking or a man staring at the surface. Usually they don't bring out the whole thing if they don't know you're coming. Or something hasn't been put back in time. That's usual.

And we're slowing down at the right place. Everybody's standing. It's the end of the line. He doesn't bother to call out the station. Why should he? So far so good. They all pick up their things, they look at each other for the first time now that they won't be seeing each other any more. They start edging toward the front end of the car through the litter of packages, magazines, bottles, not noticing, eyes fixed on nothing, thinking about what next.

All crowded up at that end. I take my bag. Why can one not go out the other way? There's no one in the aisle to stop me. I go back that way. People turn around but nobody stops me. In the vestibule the door on the platform side is closed. But the one on the other side is open. The road-bed floats past. Black stones. Black stones. Oh black stones where is it that we have floated toward each other in different circumstances? They stop. We do not know each other. Everyone else is inching out, very slowly, at the far end, onto the platform. There they are going to stop in turn in front of a little window as though they had to buy tickets over again or go through customs. That's ridiculous. I know the place. If anybody stops me. This side is right on my way. I climb down. My feet feel naked on the black stones. I cross them—a filthy beach, sloping steeply. Already the air is remarkable, though. Another set of tracks, rusty, more black stones, another set, more black stones, and then grass! I stop and put down my suitcase and breathe. I will be home tonight.

Up the bank through the long growth. Late spring. A late spring evening. Top of the bank. The trees have grown. The cushion of pine needles. Among the trash. Well, they have put some kind of pond there now! No one ever told me. The sight is depressing. I would have liked a chance to get used to the idea. It wouldn't have mattered to me, after all. If I'd known. Too late now. The pond is darker than the sky. The clouds cross it into the woods as though they'd always done that. It must seem that way now. The sun is clouded. It was the pond that did it. Or could it have been my getting off as I did? And the little window they stopped at, what was that?

An announcement? I look back. The train has already gone. The station has closed. I start around the pond with my suitcase, on the new path, but as I do I see, up among the buildings to the left, a flag start down from the top of a pole.

No, once again I will not be home tonight.

S TART with the leaves, the small twigs, and the nests
that have been shaken, ripped, or broken off by the
fall; these must be gathered and attached once again to
their respective places. It is not arduous work, unless
major limbs have been smashed or mutilated. If the fall
was carefully and correctly planned, the chances of anything of the kind happening will have been reduced.
Again, much depends upon the size, age, shape, and species of the tree. Still, you will be lucky if you can get
through this stage without having to use machinery.
Even in the best of circumstances it is a labor that will
make you wish often that you had won the favor of the
universe of ants, the empire of mice, or at least a local
tribe of squirrels, and could enlist their labors and their
talents. But no, they leave you to it. They have learned,
with time. This is men's work. It goes without saying
that if the tree was hollow in whole or in part, and contained old nests of bird or mammal or insect, or hoards
of nuts or such structures as wasps or bees build for their
survival, the contents will have to be repaired where
necessary, and reassembled, insofar as possible, in their
original order, including the shells of nuts already

opened. With spiders' webs you must simply do the best you can. We do not have the spider's weaving equipment, nor any substitute for the leaf's living bond with its point of attachment and nourishment. It is even harder to simulate the latter when the leaves have once become dry—as they are bound to do, for this is not the labor of a moment. Also it hardly needs saying that this is the time for repairing any neighboring trees or bushes or other growth that may have been damaged by the fall. The same rules apply. Where neighboring trees were of the same species it is difficult not to waste time conveying a detached leaf back to the wrong tree. Practice, practice. Put your hope in that.

Now the tackle must be put into place, or the scaffolding, depending on the surroundings and the dimensions of the tree. It is ticklish work. Almost always it involves, in itself, further damage to the area, which will have to be corrected later. But as you've heard, it can't be helped. And care now is likely to save you considerable trouble later. Be careful to grind nothing into the ground.

At last the time comes for the erecting of the trunk. By now it will scarcely be necessary to remind you of the delicacy of this huge skeleton. Every motion of the tackle, every slight upward heave of the trunk, the branches, their elaborately re-assembled panoply of leaves (now dead) will draw from you an involuntary gasp. You will watch for a leaf or a twig to be snapped off yet again. You will listen for the nuts to shift in the hollow limb and you will hear whether they are indeed falling into place or are spilling in disorder—in which case, or in the event of anything else of the kind—operations will have to cease, of course, while you correct the matter. The raising itself is no small enterprise, from the moment when the chains tighten around the old bandages until the bole hangs vertical above the stump, splinter above splinter. Now the final straightening of the splinters themselves can take place (the preliminary work is best done while the wood is still green and soft, but at times when the splinters are not badly twisted most of the straightening is left until now, when the torn ends are face to face with each other.) When the splinters are perfectly complementary the appropriate fixative is applied. Again we have no duplicate of the original substance. Ours is extremely strong, but it is rigid. It is limited to surfaces, and there is no play in it. However the core is not the part of the trunk that conducted life from the roots up into the branches and back again. It was relatively inert. The fixative for this part is not the same as the one for the outer layers and the bark, and if either of these is involved in the splintered section they must receive applications of the appropriate adhesives. Apart from being incorrect and probably ineffective, the core fixative would leave a scar on the bark.

When all is ready the splintered trunk is lowered onto the splinters of the stump. This, one might say, is only the skeleton of the resurrection. Now the chips must be gathered, and the sawdust, and returned to their former positions. The fixative for the wood layers will be applied to chips and sawdust consisting only of wood. Chips and sawdust consisting of several substances will receive applications of the correct adhesives. It is as well, where possible, to shelter the materials from the elements while working. Weathering makes it harder to identify the smaller fragments. Bark sawdust in particular the earth lays claim to very quickly. You must find your own ways of coping with this problem. There is a certain beauty, you will notice at moments, in the pattern of the chips as they are fitted back into place. You will wonder to what extent it should be described as natural, to what extent man-made. It will lead you on to speculations about the parentage of beauty itself, to which you will return.

The adhesive for the chips is translucent, and not so

rigid as that for the splinters. That for the bark and its subcutaneous layers is transparent and runs into the fibers on either side, partially dissolving them into each other. It does not set the sap flowing again but it does pay a kind of tribute to the preoccupations of the ancient thoroughfares. You could not roll an egg over the joints but some of the mine-shafts would still be passable, no doubt. For the first exploring insect who raises its head in the tight echoless passages. The day comes when it is all restored, even to the moss (now dead) over the wound. You will sleep badly, thinking of the removal of the scaffolding that must begin the next morning. How you will hope for sun and a still day!

The removal of the scaffolding or tackle is not so dangerous, perhaps, to the surroundings, as its installation, but it presents problems. It should be taken from the spot piece by piece as it is detached, and stored at a distance. You have come to accept it there, around the tree. The sky begins to look naked as the chains and struts one by one vacate their positions. Finally the moment arrives when the last sustaining piece is removed and the tree stands again on its own. It is as though its weight for a moment stood on your heart. You listen for a thud of settlement, a warning creak deep in the intricate joinery. You cannot believe it will hold. How like something dreamed it is, standing there all by itself. How long will it stand there now? The first breeze that touches its dead leaves all seems to flow into your mouth. You are afraid the motion of the clouds will be enough to push it over. What more can you do? What more can you do?

But there is nothing more you can do.

Others are waiting.

Everything is going to have to be put back.

Ends

WHEN a shoelace breaks during use the ends do not always indulge at once in their new-found liberty. However long the break may have been preparing —the threads wearing through one by one, the rub settling in the same place stride after stride, the tension mounting in the other strands, making them watchful, on guard against any further illusions—the release itself, whether it is accompanied by one of the many variants of the dull sound which in this world signifies the end of something, or comes to pass in silence, always seems sudden to the point of being unexpected. A few ends there are, it is true, which at this moment fling themselves into the air waving and disporting themselves, the result of an inherent want of substance, or simply a reaction to the long strain. Some go so far as to flap and dance as though they were now the ends of whole laces. They are usually rewarded by being removed at once and disposed of. But the better laces respond to the occasion in silence, and often do not move at all at first. Whatever their unfulfilled desires may have been, and however clearly they may have foreseen the inevitability of the parting, it is no pleasure to them to feel that they have failed to carry to its conclusion the undertaking for which they were made and upon which they had entered without reservations. The release of strain throughout these natures is likely to express itself in a sudden despondency, a disorientation, a sense of emptiness, rather than exhilaration. In this they will be reflecting the fact that with the loss of their use (for they are no longer laces—that self has gone) they have become something different, and have not yet discovered what it is. It is hard for them to relinquish a usefulness that was theirs without their having to think about it as long as they remained a whole. Their keen awareness of their fragmentary state is in itself a nostalgia for their lost usefulness. For they are still one, they are still whole, each of them, but they cannot feel that this is enough any longer, or that it will ever be enough, that it will ever have any worth, that there will ever be anything about themselves that they will value and be able to take for granted. Wherever they go next, it seems to them, they will forever feel in some part of them that they are fragments whose salvation depended upon remaining whole. They see nothing ahead of them but dissolution. Given a new self, they respond by feeling deprived of the possibility of ever having a self at all. It is possible that the self, after all, is not a matter of use. But they cling to the need to be useful as though it were a last cherished shred of their unbroken life, and very slowly and reluctantly they are drawn toward the holes and disappear around the first bends of their journeys.

The Giants

THEY were the first creatures on earth to be shod. Even those who affect to doubt their existence are silent on that point. They wrapped their feet in pieces of the world which they had made into couples shaped like their own feet, which are dedicated to The Twins, and measuring began. The statistical sense of reality, which we now live in, was their invention. As it grew they dwindled. As it took over they ceded. As it developed its voices they fell silent. As it became opaque they became invisible. As it sealed the mind they became incredible. It was their reward, it was their punishment, it was inevitable.

But it is not eternal. Give them their due, they never thought of us. They envisaged a new world, and being immortal they were aware that this is the new world, under our feet. It had to be touched in a new way. It had to be stood on differently, walked on differently. Whatever would permit this would have to be at the same time an everlasting signal of beginning, of a readiness to set out, taking its division with it. They knew they would have to give up the whole of the past.

We are still living on what they left.

But the newness of the world, where they have their home, is not only here, it keeps returning. At dawn I have seen the eastern horizon lined with pairs of immense shoes that dwarfed the mountains, waiting for the sun to fill them. They were there until I tried to count them.

Justice came later. With the bandaging of the eyes.

The Sentinel

T HEY believe that each child is invested at birth with its particular grief which will never willingly forsake it afterwards. Something more personal than a name, something in fact for which the name is a blank symbol. Something never seen by its host or by others, yet with features, a voice, a touch, that no one could mistake, even in disguise. Something that will be inseparable, for as long as he lives, from whatever each person calls "me."

Once, they say, each man was born without his grief. He was a happy nature then, little better than the animals. He was content with the earth. He was content with his body. They echoed each other. Even death was something that he gave himself up to, in due course, with a struggle that was chiefly physical, like a foot-race. He did not suspect that there was more light than he could see. Creatures from other existences came and went, passing him, but for him they were like the birds. He was not curious. He had not conceived of heaven. He did not dream. He was not complete. Only in this last detail was he already man.

It was his grief that promised to complete him, and continually renews the promise. There are many tales of how the age of grief began—the dawn of man's longing for completeness. They all agree on one point: the covenant was irreversible. There is no returning to the ungrieved world. Now that it no longer exists it never existed. The knowledge of this truth, and the nostalgia which that knowledge engenders, have become an allegory—crude, imperfect, not to be taken literally—of the yearning for heaven, but at the same time they have consolidated the rule of grief, who by now is lord of this world's past, and of its future. Any step toward the ancient precincts and their limited but untrammelled peace at once encounters a figure of dread that is one of grief's most terrible aspects, an apparition that says, "You cannot pass me. You cannot see beyond me. Even if you could there would be no sense in your triumph, for you would no longer be yourself, nor know anything, nor would heaven any longer be open to you." Between that dread and the futile (but no less attractive on that account) longing to return, some natures, indeed many natures, wither and die. Their grief surrounds them with visions of their own incompleteness. It twines around them and through them, shutting out hope, guiding them infallibly to those paths in which, as they see with relief, there is none. Toward idylls which do not exist, which is what makes them irresistible.

And still, day by day each one's grief offers to complete him, and it does not lie. That is the original promise whose acceptance was in itself a first great step on the way to its fulfilment. In its efforts toward making him complete his grief leads him into every circumstance of his existence, into every light, every premonition, every terror, every memory, into the depths of the sea, into the dark of the earth, into the cold of space, into the emptiness of the tombs, into all his echoes. It persuades him to shun happiness as a doom that does not belong to him, that is unworthy of him. It tries to lead him to the threshold at which he will bid it farewell with his whole spirit

—farewell to his grief and to all that belongs to it, and go on without it, alone, complete, into the endless present. At least for long enough so that he will know that it is possible. But only a few have ever done that, and each man's grief owns a few of their footsteps, but has made them its own. For the most part the individual severs himself from his grief only by dying. He conceives of such a parting and of his own death as the same thing, and he clings to his grief to the end as though life were nothing else. Only when he is finally dead does his grief forsake him, to enter, with undiminished hope, a child being born at that moment. For it is only the griefs of those who freed themselves in their lifetimes and attained wholeness, that are themselves free of their promise, and able to return at last to the joyful realm of their origin.

And yet each grief is no less equivocal than its host. It has hidden from him the creatures from other universes, his brothers. It has usurped or muffled their voices. It has altered or delayed their messages. It has distorted for him his sense of being alone. It has planted black flags around him and made him live in their shadows. It has covered him with its wings for fear he should see at each moment that he is already complete. Its final hold on him is to make him believe that heaven itself would be as nothing without it.

And yet his grief is a great guide through this world. Even, perhaps, the surest of the guides. As long as guides are needed. He may well be proud to remember that his grief was waiting for man as soon as man himself was made, and that in him alone it walks the earth. And which of his virtues, he asks himself, would exist for long without his grief and its promises of sadness?

But grief is merely the first, in their belief, and there is no indication that it is by any means the greatest of the guardians. And since each man has his own grief, they argue, why should he not be attended, now or in time to come, by other angels, by all the other angels, as well?

Ethel's Story

O F COURSE it was on a Monday that she decided she must have a story.

It was on a Monday because of the emptiness, in which things are known to emerge that are covered at other times. She had so little washing to do now that she was all alone, and she had got up earlier than usual to get it done, and she had got it done earlier than usual and then she had hung it out, and then she had found herself wandering down through the different back yards in which no washing was hanging yet, from which the children had just left for school. She paused at the feet of wooden stairs and listened to the sound of washing machines whirring and sloshing and the voices raised now and then to make themselves heard above the noise of the machines and she felt as though she were deaf. No one would hear her. It made no difference, she said. She must have her story.

She waited until she was back at the foot of her own silent flight of wooden steps leading up the back of the house to the upper porch where the newspapers were piled on the old sewing machine, and then she started to tell no one about her canary.

The most interesting thing about her canary had not been anything you could see in the bird at all. It had been his effect on the room he was kept in. As soon as she opened the door and looked in she could tell what state of mind the bird was in. Partly it was just the air, her first breath of it. He kept himself so clean. But partly it was something you could actually see, or at least she could, in the walls themselves. If he was feeling serene, whether or not he had been singing, the walls were bright and splashed with sunlight. If he was dreaming happily about his homeland the walls seemed to have receded; the room looked bigger and the vines and flowers on the wallpaper were clearer and seemed to stand out and look more than usually life-like. If his confinement was weighing heavily on him the walls looked dark and the patterns in the paper were lost in the featureless shadows. She would go in there and look at the room and it was better than conversing with most people, she said, how she could understand what he was feeling in himself. And so it had been until the morning when she had opened the door and the walls looked dead. Nothing on them showed any life at all. They were neither near nor far, and the light touched them as though they were only pictures of themselves. Then she had known that Dickie was dead and had gone over to the cage and found him lying on his back, stiff, with his beak slightly open.

That was the story she told, then, and she went on telling it for a long time, when no one could hear her.

When someone could hear her she told no story at all, because what had happened was that her daughter had come home to the cold house and had moved in to the room where she had grown up and had said nothing to her mother by way of explanation or by way of affection or by way of passing the time of day. She had gone out a great deal and had come home late, and she never recounted a single detail of what she did or of what she had done before. Her silence was aggressive, and her mother had always been frightened of her, and now continued to look after her, but from a distance, careful not to disturb her. Not even when she slept beyond noon. Not even when she was sick, except to take in, very quietly, a little tray of crackers and milk to set down near the bed, which sometimes were touched, sometimes not. Not even when the curtains remained closed all day and there was no sound of anyone going to the bathroom, and then they remained closed all day the next day. When panic had finally seized her she had had to go and fetch a neighbor to come back and go into the dark room and find that the girl had left without a word two days before.

The Dark Sower

Now although we say it is spring the days of glass
are assembling. Mogog the Dark Sower walks
the earth once more. For him it is the time of year—but
for him a year is a lapse that we have not learned to describe, since for us it has come only once. Is it three thousand, or ten thousand, or fifty thousand, or a hundred
thousand years? Between sowings, as the centuries pass
without his reappearance, his figure and his office are
mistaken. He becomes confused with lesser and more
sociable deities. He is portrayed as the gray god who
mildews the grain, hence as the lord of ailment. He oc-
curs on their altars with a face of smoke and they pray
to him not to be consumed. He becomes the god of ice
(more accurately) and they imagine that it is the ice
they know, and they offer him fish and birds to seize
and hold in his heart. They think of it as a heart. But
what they know of cold is no more than the shadow of
a gatehouse in his dominion. And now he has come again.

He walks at his time across the blue sky of the earth
and he sows the days of glass. They do not fall immediately. They fly out from his hand like birds settling at
evening, but transparent. With a tiny clinking like that

of sleet they congregate at a height known beforehand, which they remember from the last time. No one has disturbed their encampment. Each time as they wait they add a few improvements. They wait. More arrive. More. What a host, what a host! What a forest in the seed! The whole of the air above them and below them flocks to their camp begging to be allowed to be their banners. The sounds of the glass smithies ring day and night. The stars laugh in anticipation.

And the earth, being of that celestial ancestry, remembers this season before its creatures do. Now if you mark their places day by day you will see that stones weighing many tons have begun to move across level fields, carving deep grooves in the out-croppings, and you may be able to hear their voices—muffled rumblings and shriekings, so that you remember tales of caverns full of beards at the end of which spirits without age slept with their crowns on the tables. The roots of the trees feel a stirring and the leaves tremble on still days.

And now when you open the door at night you will see huge animals leap away into the darkness. You will think at first that they are running from you. The eland is gone in a single bound, the white of his eye flashing like a comet. The cave bear breaks away like an ice jam on a black river. The mammoth moves as though stung, a black haystack, a night sweeping across the sky. In silence. But they will not have seen you. You are no more to them than a writing on a wall. How long will you haunt the earth together?

The catastrophe they are running from never ceases but moves through the universe, recurring in its own time, whereupon the days of glass in their millions all fall together and remain, centuries of them, in a single solid sheet many fathoms deep. The animals' flight, then, is no more than a kind of cyclic worship, a dance before the event. It may consecrate them but it can never save them. The glass days fall to the earth suddenly on a spring morning when the mammoth's mouth is full of daisies.

And what of you? Do the animals run to your right or to your left? With the motion of the earth or against it? And have you saved your skins one after the other to offer to the translucent god? Have you invoked his protection each time a knife blade touched a stone, each time a glass rang? God of bells. Do you still have your little obsidian key which will allow you to enter, barefoot, the grating corridors, to pass naked by the vast halls where the animals stand like clouds, to forget each in turn, to ease your bones and your anguish through the grinding doors at last and into the head of the glass valley and hear your first bird sing, and kill the creature which does not yet know you, and laugh at the first touch of feathers, and warm your hands around its heart, and eat?

The Death-defying Tortonis

I GO OUT first now. It is a position that I am not used to in some hair-thin secret chamber on the inside of the calves of my legs, and there perhaps I will never be used to it. Perhaps no one capable of assuming the position and surviving would ever grow used to it in every part of himself. Still, I have hopes. But given the assumptions on which I base the rest of my life, including its defiance, as they say, of death, it behooves me to conceal this truth—of my not yet being wholly accustomed to my position—from the others. To whom in any event it could never be completely and continuously (because of course it is alive) and as it were luminously communicated, so that it would not, could not, contribute to their enlightenment but merely to their disturbance. I would do as well, in fact, to conceal it even from myself if I had not, in the course of the past months and years, learned to control this stubborn refusal to be accustomed, this irreducible reluctance to regard my naked position as the first rider as though it were a part of nature. Is it, in fact? But does nature defy death? I would do well not to ask such questions during the performance. The mind never despairs of escaping its own controls, even if the escape can take no form except death itself.

I go out first now. It has been two and a half, nearly three years. Four years since I began to rehearse the position. I roll the front wheel onto the wire eighty feet above the ground, with nothing below it except dark air. Dark in our eyes despite the floodlights. I feel the feet in their tights, on my shoulders. I feel the muscles in the arches of the feet contract a little. This helps me. More of my mind returns from somewhere to lend its shoulder, to hold us up. I go out only a foot or two. We go out, for they have all assembled behind me. Behind me and above me, but at this point I must not think of them as being above me. I am not sure why. It would not help. We go out only a foot or two, very slowly, as though the front wheel were groping its way along the wire to make sure it continued. At about the point where my foot on the pedal would be clearing the platform (I imagine, for obviously I do not look to see) and there is nothing under the pedal but that darkness of which the rubber of the pedal is in truth a reflection, I stop. Even more slowly we go back to the platform. They help, from behind me. And for most of two minutes we appear to be adjusting something, arranging something which, if we had not happened to notice it, would have meant certain death for all of us. We make a great display of maintaining outward calm, of showing nothing to the audience, of not betraying that anything is wrong. Those above do not even climb down but stand there the whole time with their poles, staring straight ahead, which has been found most fitting. An assistant appears to be busying himself about us. We make use of this—in fact very difficult—moment to breathe, deliberately but not in time, blinking our eyes at the top of each in-halation, at the bottom of each exhalation, until the moment when we must forget our breathing again and give ourselves solely to what we are doing. By that time the announcer far below us is announcing our act for the second time, his voice appearing to show a touch of concern, as though our false start were not a part of the act, but something unforeseen, unprecedented, and incalculable in its results. He is announcing us again but of course we do not hear it, for by then we are too far advanced in our act, its silence, its echoes. Again I move forward, the feet gripping my shoulders, gripping tighter as the back wheel, too, leaves the platform and the whole bicycle is out on the wire, the front wheel laying itself down inch by inch like a snail.

The wire. We call it a wire out of tradition rather than regard for accuracy. It is in fact a metal cable of about the diameter of an ordinary candle, enveloped over its whole length by a layer of soft rubber between an eighth and a quarter of an inch in thickness. The rubber layer has been specially applied by hand, for it is important that the bond between it and the cable should be perfect and should remain perfect. It must not slip. The outside of the rubber contains, not a coating but an admixture of sharp sand of different degrees of coarseness, which must be an integral part of the rubber layer for as long as the wire fills its present role. It would be better to have no sand at all than sand which might work loose and roll out. Or even just work loose. This is one of the things for which the wire is examined, inch by inch, after each performance. If a single grain of sand shows signs of independent movement, even though it may be nothing more definable than the first movements of a child's tooth, the whole wire is set aside, at least for repair. Naturally, when it is set up the wire is anchored to keep it from swaying.

And the bicycles. It seems hardly necessary to point out that they are not ordinary bicycles either, although everything (other than the fact that they are entirely covered with chrome, apart from the hand grips, pedals and seats) has been arranged to make them suggest the most commonplace of contemporary wheels—the low, balloon-tired sort that used to be won by selling magazine subscriptions door to door. But ours are almost as light as imported racing models. Even the girls carry theirs into the arena themselves, before the front wheels are hooked to a rope and one after the other the bicycles fly alone, straight up to the platform. (It must be their favorite moment in the whole act). There they lean against their handlers and wait. Speed would be meaningless to these constructions. But the conveyance of power from the pedal to the rear wheel is far more sensitive than it is in ordinary bicycles, for one thing. For another, the tires are not completely round but are molded with a very slight longitudinal concavity, barely noticeable when the wheels are suspended or when the bicycle is standing by itself. At such moments this conformation appears as nothing more than a flatness in the crown of the tire, scored with secondary grooves, also running lengthwise, and a tertiary hatchwork in a triangular scale pattern reminiscent of a sharkskin. A recurrent pattern —but the shark, after all, is a professional survivor. It is only when the bicycle wheel is placed on the wire, on the platform, and the weight of the rider and then the additional weight of the others presses the tire down onto the sanded envelope of the cable, that the tire yields at the crown sufficiently to produce a groove, which runs the full length of the contact. A shallow grip. Of course each bicycle is very slightly different from the others, the result of endless adjustments, some of them conceived in the small hours of the night. None of us would be able to perform with one of the other's bicycles.

So I go out first, and the image of the front wheel laying itself down like a snail did not come to me by chance. We are used to leaving nothing to chance, insofar as possible, or so we have to believe, though of course chance, chance itself is probably not even limited by our efforts. But in any case, how often that snail has appeared to me in dreams. Since I was a child. Since the days of my first slow wheel. I watched him ("him," of course, hence the intimacy of my reservations, the ready and yet awed identification) set out calmly, as though I did not exist, as though my decisions, all the rest of me and what became of all the rest of me, were eventualities too remote for him to believe in. I have even called to him in dreams and said, "Look, it's me!" But nothing. No response. Thank heaven. For I believe now that if there had been anything of the kind he would have lost some innate certainty, or I would have come to doubt it, and we would all have plunged, long since, into the abyss that awaits us everywhere.

I have allowed my mind to run at times (but never during a performance; never, in fact, when I was even touching the bicycle) on his ability to proceed equally well along the side of a wire, or underneath it, for that matter. I have dwelt with satisfaction on the image of him climbing smooth walls, crossing ceilings, negotiating intricate joints in rafters, or elaborate knots, at a great height. I have had dreams in which he disappeared—yes, disappeared, and in the course of crossing the wire in the usual way. I was the shell, or rather the bicycle and I together were the shell, or rather the bicycle and I and all the rest of us were the shell and we were suddenly filled with a weightlessness that bore no relation to anything we had practised. There we hung, a case enclosing a coil of nothing, balancing as well as we could, now that we were deprived of movement and had nothing at our center, until a tiny upward breath swept us off into the void. Naturally I have remained silent about any such images of my own. As my fellow-performers have done with theirs, if they have any, as no doubt they do.

So I go out first but it has not always been so. I am not the oldest; no, I am in fact one of the younger members of what is known, for reasons of remote pathos, as the family. Behind me the front wheel of Claudio's bicycle follows the rear wheel of mine with only a few inches between them and nothing maintaining the distance except Claudio's foot on his pedal. Claudio is eight years older than I am and wears a dark reddish toupé for the act. Tortoni is his real name. And yet he has confided to me that if he had not been put to the act so young, as we all were, he might never have chosen it. He cannot be sure but he might never have chosen it. It was one of those confidences that was surely forgotten by the person who made it almost immediately and I am sure that the thought has seldom if ever recurred to him. Claudio says very little and buys magazines about animals and nature when we have any time in a city. He is heavier than I am, heavier than any of us, but his tights always fit with wrinkles. For years, ever since I began to practice going out first, I have tried not to listen to his breathing.

It was once suggested that Claudio should go out first, but the thought troubled him so much that the idea was dropped.

Behind Claudio's bicycle comes the carefully braked front wheel of his younger brother Rafael. Rafael married Marisa two years ago, after living with her for nearly three. He is much slighter than Claudio, blond, quicker but more nervous. He worries about money. He worries about the future of the act. He reads all the papers and discusses them at large to the rest of us, usually without anyone else entering a comment. Rafael needs an abdominal operation but we hope it will wait until the end of the season because the formation as we practise it now allows of no alternatives.

Behind Rafael's bicycle comes his cousin Marcantonio's. Marcantonio's mother was a Tortoni who tried to escape the whole world of the wire by marrying outside it. But perhaps because she had never known anyone except those who performed on the wire, she chose unfortunately. The marriage was brief and wretched; she herself returned, with her child, to the familiar circumstances. Not as a performer (she had never had the temperament) but as a dresser, old before her time, controlling her pessimism with an uncertainty that led us all to keep our distance from her. Yet allowing her son to be brought up as a cyclist—her own attempt to escape the wire had exhausted her belief in any such possibility. And Marcantonio avoided her more studiously than anyone, even to having his tights made and repaired by someone else. And though the differences between our performances are almost immeasurable, it is my opinion that Marcantonio is the most reliable and sturdy of us all.

Last comes Cesare, gaunt, wiry, and no more their brother than I am. He is the son of a trapeze artist who was killed when Cesare was very small. There was no one to train him in his father's act, but Carla Tortoni, the mother of the cyclists behind me, who died last year, brought him up as a matter of course and he was put to the wire at the same age as the rest of us. His passion is dancing and he is in love with a girl who has nothing to do with any act at all, which in itself has always been thought rather unlucky. She has never seen him perform and refuses even to read the reviews of our act in the newspapers.

The feet on my shoulders belong to Augusta, one of the younger daughters. Younger than I am, and pretty. We grew up together. For a brief time in our early adolescence we slept together, until the full gravity of what we were doing dawned on us at the same time. Then we stopped without a word and without the least ill-will. Now, years later, it is good that it happened. Neither she

nor I have married. Again, one does not think of such
things during the performance.

On Claudio's shoulders the feet are Alfreddo's. He is
not a member of the family either, but a tumbler whom
they enlisted seven or eight years ago. He is the oldest
of us, married, with children whom he never sees; he is
almost the same age as Claudio's own father. He reads
one boxful of books over and over.

On Rafael's shoulders are Emilia's feet. Emilia lives
with Claudio. She is the daughter of another wire artist,
who performs alone.

On Marcantonio's shoulders, Giorgio's feet. Giorgio
is the youngest of the Tortonis, slight, small, homosex-
ual, who wanted to be a clown.

On Cesare's shoulders, Anna's feet. She is the prettiest
of the Tortoni girls, gentle, studious, and a singer.

The seats of the bicycles and the heights of the first
row of balancers have been carefully adjusted so that
their shoulders are all at the same height. This is important because when the balancers are in position a ladder
is handed up to them, through which they all slip their
heads. Then they lower it to their shoulders, which are
padded to receive it, and the ladder provides a platform,
running from Augusta in front to Anna in the rear. The
balancing poles are then handed up, and then the second
row of balancers can start to climb up, to stand on the
ladder.

Mimi first, who was a classical dancer but required
something more dangerous. She is jealous of Marisa and
everyone pretends not to know.

Then Teodoro, who is little and dark like a jockey,
and was a street urchin who used to play with us when
we were first starting to learn, and picked up the act that
way, and came with us. He is married and has five children who live with the troupe, but he is never around unless it is for some reason to do with work. He and Gior-

gio do not get along but everyone is careful not to pay any attention.

Then Maria, Cesare's sister, adopted at the same time he was. She is in love with Marcantonio, and it would be a good thing, but that is no concern of the front tire's.

Finally Ernesto Tortoni, short, neat, equable, the eldest of the sons, married without children, an impassioned and skilful devotee of the stock-market, at which he has been moderately successful over the years, considering that he started with nothing.

On the shoulders of these four, a second ladder. On which a chair is placed. Into which Graziella climbs, wearing a long gown, mock-royal, with a fluffy trim and spangles. And a rhinestone tiara. Graziella was also picked up on the street, an acquaintance of Teodoro's. She grew up with us. We first let her practise the act with us after watching her walk up a hawser into a ship, on a dare, when she was a little girl. I suppose it would be said that Graziella and I are engaged. Yes, that at least.

When we are half-way across we stop. The cyclists, one after the other, take their hands off the grips and hold them out like wings. Then each of the bottom row of balancers raises an arm. Then each of the second row of balancers raises an arm. Finally Graziella rises, climbs the chair, and unfurls a flag. We remain there, not hearing the rolled drums or the applause, for a moment, and then continue.

Everyone's role, as may be imagined, is difficult. But for the cyclists it is more difficult than for anyone, and our training began almost as soon as we could walk. Even before, if you will, with toy bicycles. We came early to regard these two-wheeled fabrications as though the world itself revolved around them. We thought of them day and night. Everything we learned led back to them at once or seemed pointless. At last we could ride. The fervor increased. We cared for nothing else. We learned

to ride more and more slowly. We learned to ride back-
ward. By pure force of concentration we learned to stop,
to remain upright in one place. Then came the moment
when an old wire was laid on the ground and we set the
wheels on it and started. When that became practicable
the first of the drops—an old tent canvas, painted—was
spread out under the wire. It represents an arena. At the
edges are the first tiers of seats, with spectators painted
sitting there, life size. We soon ceased to notice them. In
due course the wire was raised a few inches, just enough
to clear the ground. Same canvas.

Then when we were used to the raised practise wire
another canvas was spread under it. The arena was
smaller. More tiers of spectators showed. They were
smaller. As we grew more proficient the canvases de-
picted the arena and the audience farther and farther below us, until the arena looked the size of a dinner plate
and the spectators the size of hat-pins. Then a black
canvas, which was hardest of all to get used to. Then
we were ready to start learning the act itself.

But after all that, and even with luck, will we grow
much older in the act?

The audiences are not what they were even a few
years ago; our expenses are rising all the time; none of
the young seem to feel that there is a future in following
our exacting profession. Less and less people seem to believe in us, to say nothing of understanding our art.

But grandfather Tortoni says that the decline of interest has nothing to do with the world, but only with
ourselves. He says we are no longer of interest because
in fact we are not defying anything real at all. According to him we know too much, and it is all a game. Even
if we were killed we would be killed in a game. That is
what they mean when they say they don't believe we're
really doing what we seem to be doing. In contrast to
us, the old man declares that he admired his son Tom-

maso, Claudio's father, just once, when he combined risk and wit and performed on the wire, at the age of eighteen, on a unicycle, on his head. And the old man is thinking (though he is too proud to mention it) of the day when he himself drove a bicycle with a huge front wheel —an ordinary high-seated penny-farthing without special tires or anything—across a city square, a hundred feet up, without rehearsal, simply because, as he once said, "It got into him that he could." He watches us seldom, and with scorn, and he says we should turn to something we know nothing about if we are going to talk about defying death. The whole matter, he says, is far simpler than we have made it. It consists of nothing but being able to look straight ahead and see that there could not possibly be any other way.

The Visitor

Aᴺᴰ what about her, my lord, what about her? Is the kingdom of heaven only a step from her also and will the passions of the earth at a single movement of her heart fall back and bow their heads as she passes?

For seventeen years, my lord, she has come twice a week, well before the specified hours. Sundays and Wednesdays, in clean clothes with her face rubbed like an elbow and her basket heavy. To stand with the others on the far side of the street, looking up at the high black wall of the prison and the studded grilles of the windows through which shaved heads can be dimly made out, through which a hand occasionally flutters or flicks out to seize a bar as though its body had fallen from it and it was clinging to the last proof of mortal life—a prison bar —by itself. She stands there and smiles up and from time to time she waves. When the bell rings she goes over with the others to the little door by the drawbridge, between the guards' shelters, and in her turn approaches the guard who opens the door. From her basket she takes a bundle, carefully and attractively wrapped. If it is a month that bears flowers there are flowers tied to the string. The guard nods to her. He knows her. They all

113

know her. She points out the name on the bundle. He nods. She asks for news, he says everything is just the same so far as he knows, but he never sees the prisoners. He is younger than she is.

Is there any chance yet of her being able to see her husband, she asks. He looks at a board and says no. Will he not place her request before his superiors, she asks. He promises. He looks at her and says that the decision has nothing to do with him. She tells him that she knows that. She goes back and stands across the street and waves again.

From the basket she takes out a man's garment that she has been working on that season and holds it up to show the progress she has made. When the bell rings again all the hands at the grille wave and then the shaved heads disappear. She waves, the last time with a handkerchief, and goes, with the others shuffling toward the side-streets. Sometimes she returns before dusk and stands there by herself, looking up, when there is no one at the windows.

Of whose decision, made in what circumstances, is her life the consequence, my lord? Is this her first existence?

The wall by which she stands, by which she waits, is called Rumor Wall. Everyone else has heard something, whether or not it is true. Everyone else, and long ago, has heard something even about her husband but each one, my lord, and each for his own reasons, has spared himself telling her that her husband, a political suspect never in any case allowed out of his cell, was transferred to another prison some time during his fourth year and executed the following morning.

A Thing of Beauty

SOMETIMES where you get it they wrap it up in a clock and you take it home with you and since you want to see it it takes you the rest of your life to unwrap it trying harder and harder to be quick which only makes the bells ring more often.

The Second Person

You are the second person.

You look around for someone else to be the second person. But there is no one else. Even if there were someone else there they could not be you. You try to shelter in imagining that you are plural. It is a dream which the whole of the waking world is trying to remember. It is the orphan's mother who never lived but is longed for and has been accorded a pronoun that is an echo of your own, since she has no name. Her temple is an arrangement of mirrors. But nothing stays in it. Think how you keep your thoughts to yourself, on your rare visits there. And how quickly you leave.

You are the second person. The words come to you as though they were birds that knew you and had found you at last, but they do not look at you and you never saw them before, you have nowhere to keep them, you have nothing to feed them, they will interfere with your life, you cannot hear yourself, the little claws, meaning no harm, never let you alone, so tame, so confiding. But you know they are not yours. You know they are no one else's, either.

Sometimes between sleeping and waking you really

forget that you are the second person. Once again you have embarked, you have arrived, nothing is missing, nothing. The twilight is an infinite reunion. Then a messenger enters looking everywhere for someone. For the second person. Who else?

Made in the image of The Second Person, you never see your face. Even the mirrors show it to you backwards. Dear reader at times imagining in your own defense that I am the second person, I know more about you than I know about myself, but I would not recognize you. For your part, it is true that you do not know your own story. That it has all been given away. That it lies at the bottom of a river where everything joins it but no one owns it. No one admits to it. Why this elusiveness of yours, like that which lives in an animal's eye? For you have to be found, you are found, I have found you. You make a pathetic effort to disguise yourself in all the affectations of the third person, but you know it is no use. The third person is no one. A convention.

Can you never answer happily when you are addressed? Do I want you to?

No, you insist, it is all a mistake, I am the first person. But you know how unsatisfactory that is. And how seldom it is true.

The Moles

THE ants are waiting their turn. Their baggage trains
are packed in the tunnels, their soldiers know no
hesitations, their decisions are ready far in advance, and
absolute. The discipline in each of their orders is flawless, their architecture is at once a portrait of their minds
and a model of the universe with its conflicts in har-
mony. In their time we have almost ceased to exist. They
scarcely notice us, they pause, they had forgotten that
we were still here, a passing inconvenience. They move
through us without individuals, without loss, without
regret. Pain for them is a lantern signalling at a distance:
Thieves. Even when the whole of the sea has gone the
ants will not notice. When they bury us it is with a
utilitarian coldness and a finality which put those quali-
ties in ourselves to shame. The blood, the brains, the organs they pile above the spot, after changing them back
into red earth. They use only the veins, gradually im-
proving everything beyond recognition. They descended
from the sun, live on fire, fear nothing else. They are
farther from us, with their great heads, than any star.

But the fate of the moles is linked to our own, and to
the sea's. They are not waiting for anything. They seek

tirelessly for new places to ask us whether we are who we are, and if that is enough. Each time that we are led at last to lie down in green pastures they raise near us their little mounds that are models of our graves. Is this dust yours, they say? Confronted with silence they raise another one, a lost city in the twilight. Is This Yours, is its name. Is this the one you will return to? Is this the one you were made of? Is this you—the rest of you, which you left behind? If this had been taken up in the same hand, and the breath of life had breathed into it the same command, and it had come with you, would you be whole now, would you be at peace? The stars come out. New hills rise around us. More lost mothers. Once again we become part of the darkness. It is not too late. The moles, propelled by a small model of the forgotten sea, with eyes for nothing but their labors, urge their black bones forward in our endless quest.

The Islands

THE islands always disappeared.

After a long time men learned to build their own islands. Then men too began to disappear. There were more and more men all the time and the faster there were more of them the faster they disappeared.

Under the sea there lived an old man bent over like a bell, who could hear pain. He could hear the pain even of those who disappeared. He could hear the pain of disappearance itself, of which night is one form and day another. He could hear the pain which those who disappear left behind. There was nothing he could do. All suffering flowed into the sea and the weight of the sea rocked on his ear-drum. His breathing made the waves. When he saw the moon he was reminded at once of how everything was and he sighed, and the tide turned once more. The worst thing was that he could not tell whether the pain he heard was from the past, the present or the future, for pain was already time's keeper.

It is because I forget, he said. If I did not forget things they would not disappear. He tried to remember. The pain grew worse. And everything, as it disappeared in the sea after all his efforts, was still crushed into one terrible syllable that sank straight toward him. It is because I know too much, he said. And he tried to forget. But the whole sea shook him to remind him, bringing the echoes.

If there is no hope for me perhaps I can help someone else, the old man said, for he was a good old man. For his own sake and for theirs he tried to find someone who knew nothing about pain. At last he gathered around himself the unborn and in a very low voice began to tell them stories about the islands.

Blue

I N THE deepest part of blue one of the immortals lives
alone.

There is almost no light so he sits outside. His vast
eyes—two moonless, starless, windless nights across
which the same clouds are passing—never close. At
long intervals one of them re-visits the world of the spec-
trum and is a night again. (The other never leaves him.)
Even then the two remain one in his mind. While they
are apart all dreams cease except the dreams of frogs,
toads, and fish—cold dreams, like his own, full of shadows, with no future. It is only when his voyaging eye is
away that he himself dreams. All that appears to him
during such eclipses delights him, and his memory is
composed of nothing but remnants of those nights full
of the silence of antiquity.

The recurrence of one of them is announced by the
darkening of a rainbow. A shadow appears on the blue
edge and deepens. A line of violet, almost black, bends
upward into the sky. It spreads across the iridescent path,
washing each zone with blue, then darkening. Finally
the almost black rainbow rises until it fills the sky. That
night we lie empty of everything, dreamless, while the

toads sit hypnotized by the drumming of their hearts.

There is no pity in him. Where would he have learned it? The dead drift past him in their gray boats but he never knew them.

But there is no harm in him. Over his door, where no mortal eye could read anything, it is written, "We Are All Children Of The Light."

The Songs of the Icebergs

Ｏne at a time, one at a time, men have been favored
with the sound, even sometimes at great distances, or at night, or in fog. In almost every case they
have spent the rest of their lives cherishing their disbe-
lief. Or so it has been at least since the invention of print-
ing—a day, after all, in the saga of the ice. And the
legends—mermaids and sirens were easier to accept, for
their faces could be seen, their mirrors, their hair, their
hands extended in gestures out of the dreams of men. It
required consistent deliberation to deny them souls, to
banish them from the plausible world door by door. The
songs of the icebergs never entered it except as a cold
breath. After which one of those who had felt it would
be seen, perhaps, with the look of a man who is surprised
to find himself in possession of an incomprehensible and
inexpressable secret.

The songs have even been seen more often than they
have been heard, but then it has been easy not to recognize them. They have taken the form of illuminations
rising from within, toward the surfaces of the leprous
cliffs, like the northern lights themselves still searching
for them, or like arms and faces drowned in slow rivers,

appearing and then sinking again, to reappear farther along.

Those white mountains are far from home. What can they do but sing? The water, and the habits of our own ears, distort the sound so that what usually reaches men seems to be nothing but a series of creakings, splinterings, gnashings, occasional screams—emanations to which the hearer, with the familiar door-shutting movement to which he believes he owes his very identity, hastens to deny any vestige of intention, plan, form, spirit. And yet the whales, who are imprisoned in no such rigid refusal, though they themselves have been able to catch only occasional chords from the pale submerged hillsides, have built on their recollections the whole of their rich and happy music. And from still fainter refrains the porpoises have shaped their delicate carols.

Yet the songs of the icebergs are tragic. That is why they come to men only to be turned away. Much as man wants pain, this one he knows he dare not welcome lest it prove to be his. He shuns it as though his very teeth had begun to sing and sleep had threatened never to touch him again. For this is a strain of the great singing. None is more bereft, none more lonely, none more hopeless. The icebergs, floating in a stunned peace that moves slowly toward the bright rim of the earth, are mercilessly shattered by their own destiny. All their whiteness was born of the dark, all their fires were lit by the cold at the ends of the earth. From their depths to their summits they were brought up to silence. They might have stayed there in perfect peace until time had died. But there was a flaw in the whiteness. It was in love with the light. And with unspeakable pain it set out to reach the sun, forsaking everything else forever. However the planet turned it continued its journey, gathering to itself a few ghosts, a few bones, a few echoes of bones, a few curses, a voice. Crossed by a few white creatures. Unconsolable. Breaking. That is in the songs.

SHORTLY before dawn he burrows into the sky and begins to sing. One by one the stars turn to the other side to hear him, and their light leaves ours and fixes on the small black insect singing of the world that they will never see because it is on the side from which they have turned. As long as it is day here he sings to them and we do not even hear him. And as soon as our light has gone he stops and comes out and sits on the sky, having done his work, and then they turn one by one and try to see the world of which he has been singing. All night their faces burn through the darkness, empty but hoping.

The Remembering Machines of Tomorrow

THE human memory is a wonderful development but its fallibility is infinite. How can it be left to men? It has forgotten even its own story—the whole of evolution. It does not recall why the spirit of man walks with a limp. It can no longer say why, through a landscape of peace, fatness, and fragrance, his for the taking, of sumptuous birthplaces with meals already set, fires already lit, welcomes prepared for no one but him, he forces his bitter mouth and his naked hands farther and farther into his hunger, his cold, his namelessness, his desolation. What triumph will he recognize, what wind will he acknowledge, what sky will he warm for long? Everywhere he dreams of a creator who remembers, and he continues the search for Him, hoping that in the end what he will find will be himself. But whenever he moves he forgets something. Whatever he adds to himself he adds at the same time to the void which gnaws at his organs—all of them. It is this gnawing, and no hunger that he shares with the rest of the creatures, that drives him from them. He listens to the gnawing as though it were a song, and goes on, forgetting even that. How could things be left in such hazard? When he has finished forgetting the past he will have no choice but to start on the future. He has started already. No, it cannot go on.

Fortunately he still has his thumb, the inventor, and even before the problem has been clearly stated (oh, long before that) he has contrived the first steps toward its solution. The distance from the first notches bruised into bark, which were the ancestors of numbers, to the air-conditioned archives of the age of history, represented only a few strides in his ignorant progress, a day in his forgetting. But once there, he noted with a certain shame that everything seemed to have left him to hide in the intricate halls, where he could not again feel that it was really his, though the halls had been designed by minds like his own. His own story had now forgotten him. No, it could not be left at that either.

Faced before with crises he had developed his other thumb, named (by him) Sacrifice. At each movement of utter risk he had held up this shell-faced totem and offered part of himself in exchange for—often that has been forgotten. What was given up was presumably given up forever, but not all at once. The payment might be spread over a long time. He gave up his legs for the wheel. He gave up the strength of his arms for the lever. He gave up power after power of his physical form. And now at last, as more and more was forgotten, he began to relinquish his memory so that something would be remembered.

Since the great primitive repositories had been impersonal, and what he took to be their codified memories seemed to have less and less to do with what he still remembered as himself, a new link was needed.

The rest of this does not allow of the past tense.

The first of the remembering machines is immense, immobile, no one's. It learns, that is true. But its learning is based on information fed into it by sophisticated procedures, consciously, voluntarily. It is constructed of fragments. Even though it can record anything about us that we can conceive of having recorded, it is still in the main a recorder, rather than a memory. But its progeny is approaching us.

The machines will become, in time, more compact. They will become the pride of smaller and smaller institutions, the playthings of more and more of the privileged. They will no longer retain mere symbols in an arbitrary system, but something which can pass, at least, for whole experiences—intellectual, sensual, visionary. The process—not so much of remembering as of confronting a memory recorded with mechanical objectivity, will be painful of course, but that has not proved an insuperable obstacle in the past and is not likely to do so in the future. It will be construed as part of the new sacrifice. And the development of the remembering machines will come to be regarded as an important next step in man's evolutionary progress—something at once inevitable and worth anything it might cost. When the machines become small enough so that every person can have—then must have—his own, the day will be celebrated as the beginning of a new age of The Individual.

The machines will retain, in flawless preservation (though the completeness of what they remember will occasion some dispute, for a time) not only what their owners experience but what their owners think they have experienced, and will sort out the one from the other. More and more, such distinctions will be left purely to the machines. And it will be noticed that the experience to be retained is itself becoming a dwindling fauna, clung to by sentimentalists, from afar, who still lay aside their machines for days at a time and secretly yearn for the imaginary liberties of the ages of forgetting.

The simplification of private experience will be more

than made up for by the rapid improvement of communication among the machines themselves. It will be possible to share more and more fully the memories of others. The memories of the dead will be available in the new repositories, and many will be privately owned. With the universal recognition of the therapeutic benefits and the practical advantages of a precise memory, children will be fitted with these devices at birth. Their pre-natal experiences will have been picked up and played into their first sets. They will be given new ones as they grow older and can use them. The stages of such use will seem to reveal a new pattern in the growth of the individual and hence of the species. What man is will seem to be on the point, once again, of harmonious emergence.

Then here and there a ghost will be seen. Someone who has lost his machine. The terror he engenders will be discussed, collated, contained. It will be comprehensible, though the ghost himself no longer is. The apparition will be accorded its place, and will not long trouble those who still have their machines—any more than if, in the old days, they had seen some mutilated creature begging in the street, in the service of his unimaginable life. Little by litle it will be remarked, but with a mathematical coolness, that experience is not only flowing into the machines but that they, to an increasing extent, are becoming its source as well. Man's experience of the mechanized memory of his experience—that is what will fill more and more of his days on earth. Until, apart from the simplest bodily functions, his new life will come to revolve around nothing but the operation of the machines themselves. The memory of old risks will return, but faintly, vaguely, and so crudely that he cannot take them seriously. For perfection will seem to be in sight at last. Attached to every person like a tiny galaxy will be the whole of his past—or what he takes to be the whole of his past. His attachment to it will constitute the whole of his present—or of what he takes to be the present. The neat, almost soundless instrument will contain all of each man's hope, his innocence, his garden.

Then one by one, but with growing frequency, men will begin to lose their machines.

What We Are Named for

To say what or where we came from has nothing to
do with what or where we came from. We do not
come from there any more, but only from each word
that proceeds out of the mouth of the unnamed.

And yet sometimes it is our only way of pointing to
who we are.

The Billboard

WHENEVER he asks they tell him the same thing. They are going to give him something for the use of his place, once they have finished investigating his title to it. As he understands them, it won't be a lump sum. Actually he'd settle for a lump sum but he thinks it's shrewder not to admit that. It will be more like rent, dealt out to him at intervals for the rest of his life. He can see how they stand to gain by such an arrangement. At his age they might not have to go on paying for long. Still, as he reminds himself, after that it won't matter to him. And it had never occurred to him that he might end his days with a pension. Anything at all would be better than his present position. No income at all. Living on what he can find, down in the streets. Making his way back up, in the evening, to the shed, where he can shut out the dogs. Where he used to be able to shut out the dogs.

The investigation, to tell the truth, is taking longer than he'd expected from what they'd told him at first. But he's not seriously worried. He has a better title to his place than most of his neighbors, in the thousands of sheds on the hills around the city, have to theirs. He's been there longer. He's kept women there, raised children, pigs, chickens. It's probably taking them so long to investigate because it was so long ago that he came there and built the shed and brought the first of the women up to the place. It had a good view, and at that time he and she used to like to sit in the doorway and watch the lights in the city, before going in to bed. That's one thing he regrets, a little. The billboard they are putting up on his place is gradually shutting out the view of the city. But he tells himself that that's a trifle compared to ending your days with a pension. It isn't as though his eyes were much good any more, anyway. If he sat in the doorway now, even if the sign weren't there, all he'd see would be a blur. They're shutting out part of the sky, too, but with a pension he could buy a hammock and lie outside looking up.

Recently he has been inquiring more often about the progress of the investigations. Not just because the inquiry seems to be taking longer than he had expected, and he would prefer to start on his pension while he might still be able to enjoy it, but also because the construction of several of the supports for the billboard has forced the construction workers to demolish parts of his shed. Every evening when he comes back he finds that more of the building has been ripped down to make way for the beams and trusses and pits filled with concrete that are to anchor the high wooden wall in the heavy winds that sweep through the valley. The dogs get in through the wide jagged openings now, and eat or run off with whatever he leaves there. He drives them out when he comes home and barricades the openings as well as he can with the sticks and rubble that have been torn down from the walls of his shed. It would be a help if he could use some of the materials left over from the construction work. But the new materials, naturally, are locked up, and in any case they'd notice at once if he ever managed to incorporate any of those in patchwork construction of his own. And the odds and ends left over after a day's work are either burned on the spot or carted away in trucks. Whenever he asks it's explained to him that there's a law which forbids them to let him have any of those things. And they will not allow him to attach his repairs to the sign supports. Every morning they knock down anything he has built which touches or gets in the way of their construction.

And every day less remains of the shed. But he still lies in a corner at night, holding his stick to beat off the dogs, telling himself that the billboard will be a fine windbreak, and that the investigations cannot be far from completion now, because the workmen have nearly finished the enormous sign which will tell the whole of the city what to want.

The Conqueror

I have not always been like this," he said. "At one
time my performance did not call up vibrations out
of the Great Fault. On the other hand I was not remembered for so long."

Here I thought of the sound of the stadium as I had
approached it, when the sport had already been going
on for heaven knows how long. The air had been oppressive around the walls, like a held breath, and I had
been unable to tell whether the shrieking that rose from
inside was an expression of the excitement and pleasure
of the spectators, or the monosyllable of some ultimate
terror.

"This is by no means the first time it has happened,"
he went on, "but so far no one has been so hypocritical
as to destroy my statue or change my name on the boule-
vards, and they will not do so this time, never fear.
Though even if they did, it would not make much difference, in the long run. As it is, look at the size of my
name on the posters. Each time I take the field I am their
idol. What they would all like to be, to be loved by, to
know. How they smile on the little boys, who are happy
to admit it. Then the anthemn is sung. The adversary

comes forward, all flutes, flowers, little songs. I draw my sword. The match begins. I used to have to send back reports. Everything took longer. Except the game itself."

"After the beginning, one forgets the spectators. One forgets time. One plays as well as one can, aware for the moment of nothing else. One wins, and turns in one's bloody boots to see that the spectators have changed. Everything about them looks different, and they are on their feet, shrieking, not in admiration but in disgust. They cry now for vengeance. They grieve over what I have done to please them. If only I were alive, they say, so that I might be punished! Imagine! Pretending that I am not alive!"

I said, "In my own part of the stadium it is not so much the killing they object to, as the pleasure it gives."

"They won't escape that, either," he said, "merely by building larger stadiums, with worse acoustics, as they're doing at present. The only way for anyone to get home is to go with the crowd. Those who leave before the show is over, either singly or by twos and threes, though the party were to include the president himself, are met at the gate, where they are covered with flowers, presented with flutes, and given little songs to memorize."

The Locker Room

THIS time no one told us anything. We do not even know where the battle was, on which our fates depended. But there is not a word of surprise as we find ourselves, at our age, being herded down those iron stairs to the pale green foyer lit with naked bulbs. Bulletin boards. Frosted glass windows and doors. One of the big windows open, revealing several men younger than we are, in white smocks, seated or standing at desks, among filing cabinets. We are kept waiting. There are no benches. We look around to see who we know. We see a face we recognize, and we smile little wincing smiles, but then wonder whether we should indicate that we know anyone there at all, and from then on we stand still, saying nothing, feeling our stomachs like dark ships slowly sinking. We are told to take off our shoes. Keep the socks on. We stand holding our shoes, watching how the others hold theirs, without meeting eyes. Yesterday this time, or even two hours ago, we were being deferred to in positions of relative eminence. Our modesty became us. Almost certainly it became us. We deprecated. And quite genuinely: aware that the esteem in which apparently we were held exceeded our deserts. Yes, but we did not stand in our socks, with our shoes in our hands, waiting, on a cement floor that was not quite dry, smelling the shoes, the socks, the floor, something else, and beyond double frosted doors the unlit locker room. Some of us, clearly, had taken no exercise for years. Some were perspiring. Some seemed to be looking for things in their pockets. It's true that we'd been picked up without warning, and just as we were. Told we would need nothing else. Probably no one knew where we were. A clever-looking young man, growing bald already, hurried out from the room with the desks. His white smock billowed around him and he was carrying a clip-board from which sheets of paper struggled to detach themselves and fly away across pallid horizons, where they would settle quietly on vast plains, in the spring twilight, two by two. He opened the locker room doors, switched on the yellow bulbs inside, and motioned us through, checking off each of our names as we passed him, and giving each of us a little string with a tag on it, bearing a locker number.

The strings were dirty.

"Don't put the tags in your mouths," he told us, though no one seemed tempted to do so. And we filed past, holding shoes in one hand, tag in the other, and began to drift and eddy up and down the rows of lockers, a slow yellow-lit tide backing up into an old harbor. Then the sound of the first tin locker-doors. A few voices, laughing a little at having found them. Striking up new acquaintance, with an effort at jocularity, even at such a time, in such a place. And the smell of the lockers. The care with which hand after hand hesitantly sets about undoing its necktie. And there are no hangars for suits which have always had hangars. Years ago we did not have suits that were used to hangars. The ones we have come in with hang uncomfortably on the snub hooks, and at once dust seems to have begun to settle on them. Out of the corners of our eyes we see garters, and white calves, and white shirt-tails, and then shirts fluttering into the lockers like guilty things, but all we hear is an occasional creaking and snapping of joints, heavy breathing, wheezing, sniffing, a stifled moan. And the squeaking and banging of the locker doors. Pale sides of skin emerge to right and to left, bending, patting, sighing. Some of us must have had no exercise for years. Some of us plainly have had no exercise for years. Some of us obviously have revealed our birthday suits only to the bought bulbs of bathrooms, for years. The young man with the clip-board moves along the aisles, checking. He tells us to hang the tags on the locker doors when we are finished, and then close the lockers and stand with our backs to them. There is a muttering. Some are saying prayers. The smell of us grows stronger than that of the old locker room, but when I look up at the ceiling I can imagine that we are still as we once were, years ago, standing under those same yellow tiles, with no hair on our cold privates, shivering, and I cling to that image.

Almost all of the locker doors must have shut, and almost all of the abdomens must have turned slowly, the shoulders squaring a little, the eyes seeking out some spot on the locker across the aisle, when another clever-looking young man with a clip-board comes through the doors and confers with the first one. They speak together in low tones for a moment, comparing their papers. Then the first young man nods and straightens.

"As you were," he says. "Get dressed."

The sigh. The sound of bodies falling as one or two faint. The fumbling with the lockers. The underwear. Feeling tight. Feeling clammy. The shirt. Feeling dirty. And too small. The trousers. Feeling tight. And short and strange, and looking different in the light. Yes. They've grown old. Very old. As old as though we'd been standing there for years. Or as though they'd been hanging there since we were children. And the jackets. Much too small, too short in the arms. And old. With holes in some of the pockets. And in others nails. Clasp-knives. Crumpled pieces of paper which we remember but about which we say nothing. The socks. Dirty, fished from among several dirty pairs. The shoes. Sneakers. Too small. The first young man with the clip-board is going among the aisles telling us to hurry. The wallets. Almost nothing in them but our names. The sound of somebody sniffing again. And the first young man with the clip-board and the billowing smock, leading us rapidly down a green hall that echoes like an inner-tube, to the gymnasium, where samples of our blood, our urine, our hair, are collected. And then the safety doors clanking open and the cold air of the recreation ground, where we are released—yes, released—one by one and allowed to walk away in silence, past the new windows.

The Answers

You knock once more, wondering whether they will recognize you, after so long. Probably they will not know you on sight. Now what if a window flies up, farther along the narrow street, and a crabbed old woman puts her head out to ask you what you want? How will you find a few plausible words suitable for shouting to an upper window when you would, to tell the truth, prefer not to be overheard?

How can you say, "An answer"?

Then what if she asks your name, as she almost certainly will? You will pretend, for many reasons, not to have understood, and knock again?

"But they don't live there," she will call at last, indignant, just as you notice that the house is directly across the street from the police station. Adding, "And they never lived there."

It's true, there's not a sound inside and there's no name beside the door.

What if she asks, "What did you want to see them about anyway?" Can you really shout back, "That's one of the things I hoped they'd know."

But by then the night air will have started to wake

and stretch in the shadows, and she will have clutched her soiled shawl around her neck and shut the window.

"And yet everything in the world," you insist as you go down the steps, "still has its door."

Tribesmen

NOTHING about us impresses them. They walk into a town, emaciated, hollow-eyed, and very tall, and they look around as though they doubted whether we or anything that is ours had three dimensions. They laugh at our weapons even when they die of them. They brush our buildings with their fingertips, then they look at the fingertips, catch each other's eyes, and shrug.

They say that the only enemy worth overcoming is shame. This spirit assumes a different form, so they believe, in each generation. He is overthrown sometimes for good, sometimes for evil. He himself is neither. He is Non.

But nothing belongs to him. He is merely a guard. And a liar, like most guards. They respect no one who is his dupe or his lackey. But they revere only those who have advanced boldly and alone into the very domain he has been set to keep watch over—the country of Non—and there have seen at last, reflected in the sky, the walls of light, and have glimpsed the beginning of the crystal stairs.

Greeting to Be Addressed to the Dead
on the Morning of Their Fifth Year

I T IS your day, patient one.

We would hardly know it was you, under the rags. Pieces from last year, a belt from the year before, remnants of boots from the year before that, even some buttons and rusted fastenings that must hark back to the ill-fitting narrative you were buried in. Everything that we have brought you year by year, please note, has been true to what you might have been, insofar as we have been able to imagine that. Look, we have brought you your new story.

The hat with the bright feathers was a gift from the king of the winds, a token of esteem and an invitation to meet and to be loved by his daughter, the most beautiful princess in the empire. You are on your way to his domains. The whole of the night is your guard. The blind are drawn up along your road. As you pass each one he sees the sunrise. These flowers, now, are to give to her when you see her. And these are to give to her the day after. And once again this ribbon which we wrap around you recounts the days of your happiness and of our hope.

You that were poor. You that were ignorant. You that were graceless and ungifted and frightened and cold of heart.

This year you will find us again in your story. In great need. Remember us. Bless us out of your superabundance. Wake us with hope. See, we leave you every colored thing we have brought with us, and turn back in our black garments to what we have inherited and call the truth. To history, the form of despair reserved for the living.

Noon

He who is wearing the helmet of Death is walking at the foot of the walls. The shadow of the enormous casque falls over his body like a bell. He lets others do his shouting for him. No one shouts, wearing the helmet of Death. He turns. He waits.

Around him the empty plain, and the dead, who have taken the form of doors, each standing by itself, locked, with no shadow. Large birds alight, bringing their own shadows to walk on, and disappear behind the doors. He is wearing the helmet of Death.

While he wears it no weapon can touch him, no sound can startle him, no sight can move him.

No one dares fight with him. The silence is his triumph.

But Death has missed the helmet.

The Daughters of Judgment

OVER the door the central figure is not God, neither the Father nor the Son, but Judgment himself. Here is suffering in the stone. His eyes, one must suppose, are somewhere in the shadow under his forehead. It is not possible to say whether they are fixed on anything.

Around the portal in orderly multitudes are carved the daughters of Judgment, each of them with her deformity—one with one eye, one with none, some with no hands, some with no feet, several with no legs, many with no heads. After each of his decisions a daughter was born to him. Many, many daughters, each as far short of perfection as his decision had been.

And this is Judgment himself, for whom they were named, and from whom we are descended.

Companion

A FEATHER has been following me all morning, like a little dog. One laughs at such moments, mumbling something about knowing what that means. Of course one does not, but it is better to suggest that one does, and has made one's arrangements. It was lying there on the rug when I got up. A small gray breast feather, curled like a lock of hair. I could see the down trembling, though I could feel nothing, myself. When I put on one of my shoes it came forward. I thought that perhaps the shoe and the feather were joined by something—a hair, or a spider's thread—and I passed my hand between them. Nothing. As I walked away the feather skimmed along behind.

It followed me down the stairs. Do I make that much wind, I wondered. I went more slowly. It did the same. It followed me back up the stairs again.

I tried to catch it. Hoping no one would ask what I was doing. That led nowhere. And I felt that I would have offended us both if I had continued.

But I did try to drop clothes over it. It knew that trick too. It followed me, when I left, over grass, across the road, among animals, through the rain. I wondered whether anyone noticed. Sooner or later, I thought, and tried to imagine how long it would be possible to laugh about it, and what would be said after that.

But it does no harm. When I sit down it settles a little way off, sometimes out of sight. When I get up it's there behind me again. Does it want anything from me? Does it know anything? Who is it obeying, and why? Will it ever say? Has it come to help, to betray, or simply—as one hopes—to please itself?

One gets used to things, and in the end one does not want them to go.

Where Laughter Came from

LAUGHTER was the shape the darkness took around the first appearance of the light. That was its name then: The Shape The Darkness Took Around The First Appearance Of The Light.

The light still keeps trying to touch its lips. The lips of darkness.

The light's hand rises but the darkness is not there. Only laughter.

The Cliff Dance

It is dangerous to look back down the cliff. But the cliff above is invisible until it has been touched. Below, it can never be touched again, but at least it can be seen, however distorted from this angle.

And I must look at something besides the eternal clouds, their shadows, the wings that flash past like swords in the ceaseless battle that is only occasionally comprehensible. The cries, the cries! To think that I once cried like that, and gave it up for these hands, these words, this weight and this strangeness, from which everything is made, and knowledge emerges.

Looking down I hang in my own throat like a clapper in a bell. Oh let the hour not catch me at this, nor prayers, nor fires, nor funerals. Wind, stop and think. We are all trying to do something that is beyond us.

Below me, however the rock face changes, the pattern of the holes where I have clung to it repeats itself over and over, climbing. Out of the infinite patterns available to two arms, two legs, the same star has been discovered again and again, climbing. I see the story. From the foot-holes and hand-holes to which I will never return, life and death are pouring. From one a trickle of water. From one a beam of light. From one birds coming and going to feed their young at that height. From several a thread of smoke. From many a hollow sound, groaning and whistling. From many a splash of blood.

Steps of the dance.

I am dancing.

The Barriers

OFTEN I would wake being told that I had never been asleep, that I had seen every red light appearing in the darkness and had called out in time to warn the driver in his ink-blue coat which I secretly believed was black, and the black hat which he wore to some meetings and to some funerals, and which smelled of cold. My warnings jarred the three old women nodding on the velvet seats, admiring their circumstances in the darkness, shivering from the cold, feeling their brooches, and one or other of them, in the beginning, was sure to say to the driver, and then to the others, "See, he hasn't been asleep."

I was sitting, in short pants, on top of the glove box, so that I had to bend down to see out ahead and speak up when I spotted a red light and often I would wake being told that I had never been asleep but had heard every word of the driver's telling the three old women in their hats like black wedding cakes that this was the best hour for driving, when no one was on the roads. Now was when time could be made. The darkest hour. The hour before the dawn. The psalmist's hour. The hour for which we were all old enough. The hour of no music.

The hour of no birds. The hour of slate, of washed slate, of washed slate, of slate rising washed and drying, in which we are rising, making time. Often I would wake shivering and dropping forward and being told that I had never been asleep and hearing how we had made some time already, and peering ahead to see whether there were more lights to be discovered, and seeing the shadow of the car rise up out of the ditch like a kid-napper in clothes that had been given to him and totter alongside on the bank, running to keep up with his peaked cap, and pitch forward even so, and fall full length, face down into the ditch once more, only to rise, over and over, as often I would wake and be told, and see ahead of us the barriers striped black and white, sometimes hung with yellow lights, but usually with none, and I would speak up then too, but be greeted with silence.

Then we would turn, to the sound of slowing down, and the barrier would veer beside us, flashing black and white, and the driver would say that that was just one more reason to travel at that hour—because we were re-freshed, which was all to the good, since there was al-ways the unforeseen but we would make time even so. I did not know any name for the barriers. Each time that was the same. They appeared again and again, but when I spoke up saying that they were there, there was no an-swer until they were past. Then the driver would say something about the hour again and how we would make time even so.

Often I would wake being told that I had never been asleep, and the light was seeping into the sky, the shadow of the car had stopped rising and prowling and falling, the lights were growing faint and beginning to look naked, and the board fences painted in stripes of black and white were nowhere to be seen. Already they had been caught up into the gray. No one remembered them.

No one wanted to refer to them. But I would wake having seen them, having never been asleep, while the old women lurched, time was still being made, and we went on toward day.

What Happened While They Were Away

THE ——s (they were quite real, they are quite real,
they were well-known in that section of ——,
which is the name of the town, they were even what is
known as respected, even very respected, and if I do not
give their name it is not because I do not know it but
because on the contrary they are terribly real, and they
might be hurt. More important, they might sue me.)
The ——s were supposed to be away for the summer. I say they were *supposed* to be away for the summer. And they were away for the summer, but someone
had been left behind. He thought there never had been
such an empty afternoon. There was not a flower in the
parched garden. They had all been put away. There
were no passers-by to greet, naturally, because everybody had heard that the ——s were away. In the vacant lot next door the dust had its own games, but he did
not know anybody there. Everybody seemed to have
changed. And the whole summer stretched ahead. Meanwhile the present was empty all the way up to the sky.
And then he noticed that something seemed to have happened to everything he could remember. It was no
longer solid. He did not dare watch. Bitterly he turned
his eyes away.

Those with stronger characters may disapprove. He
felt he had no choice. He made his way down into the
cellar. Mr. ——— always said "Are you sure you've
locked the cellar door?" but he made his way down for
all that. Oh the summer light through the cobwebs on
the cellar windows, resting fondly on the faded labels of
the endless cans of peas bought wholesale, years before,
at a discount, and on the equally faded labels of numer-
ous larger cans of sauerkraut, bought in bulk, years before, from an acquaintance, and on the labels, faded only
at the ends of the boxes, of soap flakes, bought in quantity, years before, at a saving, from an advertisement,
and on the yellowing labels of dark red jars containing
home-made jams—their ink now turned the color of
iodine, and their labels like turned-up eyes of people lying on their sides trying to remember. So! The cupboard
doors were open. This was what happened when the
———s backs were turned! Nothing seemed to be missing (though how could he tell?) but there were signs. A
person had been there. Perhaps was still there! Yes, he
could see: it was an old woman. There were her overshoes. She kept them out here. There was her umbrella.
Old woman's umbrella. He was on the scent now. He
listened, which of course he would have done well to do
in the first place. From the inner room, the boiler room,
he distinctly heard sounds coming—sounds repeated
over and over, like the faint rasping of a broom on a hollow paving stone, but quicker. Like a broom in sand, but
quicker. More like a quiet hooting, like someone breathing all the time through a tube. Of course he went in. But
he went in slowly. So that his eyes would be able to set
themselves down in the darkness in there without mishap.

But it was not as dark in there as he had expected it to
be. It was the boiler and the coal bins that gave the impression that it would be dark. Beyond them the light
was quite good considering that no one was at home.

And there—he had been absolutely right—was the foot of an old woman's bed, with the shape of an old woman's feet under the old quilt. Sitting bolt upright in the bed, with her shawl around her shoulders, was a skeleton, and sitting on two bentwood chairs beside the bed, very close to her, with their backs to him, were two skinny men, shaking and making the sound that he had heard. He stood there, and they went on making the same sound. He could not tell whether they were laughing or crying. He edged around toward the light to get a better look, to see whether he could see any tears. (He remembered that was always the first thing to do.) When he got to where he could see their faces, which were very skinny indeed, he still could not see any tears. On the other hand he still was not sure whether they were laughing or crying. They never looked up, never seemed to notice him. They were gazing the whole time at the skeleton's face. It was awkward. With the ———s away. He was not quite sure what to do next. He was not sure how far his responsibility could be said to extend. He cleared his throat. Still the two skinny men paid no attention to him, sitting there with their hands on the edge of the bed, leaning forward to look into the skeleton's face. Well, in the end he went right up to one of them and said, "Excuse me," and started to feel his pulse (which he had finally remembered is always the next thing to do).

It was only then that the skinny man turned to look at him. The other went right on watching the skeleton.

"Excuse me," said someone, "but I only wanted to see if you were alright."

The skinny man just stared at him.

"The ———s are away, you know," someone said. Still no answer. The same blank stare. The other skinny man still paying no attention, and both of them still shaking and making that sound.

Then the one whose pulse was being felt stopped making the sound. He looked at someone. "It's too late," he said.

"Yes," someone agreed. The skinny man's pulse seemed weak and rapid.

"The ———s are away," the skinny man told him in a dazed voice. What he said came from a long way off. He went on. "So we made our way down here." There were signs that another person—yes, it was an old woman—had come down ahead of them. Appeared to have moved right in. They had seen her overshoes. Old woman's overshoes. And her umbrella. Old woman's umbrella. Though it had not been raining for weeks. Then they had heard a sound in the boiler room, like a sighing. So of course they had gone in. It was not as dark as they would have expected. And there she was, a very old woman lying in the bed. She had asked them what they wanted and they had told her that the ———s were away and that they had made their way down here. She had said that she knew that the ———s were away. Well, they had told her, they would go now and not disturb her. But then she had asked them not to go, please. Please not to go. So they had stood looking at her.

Then she had asked them whether they could see alright and they had told her that they could see fine, thank you. So she had told them to bring their chairs over by the bed. They didn't have any chairs but they had found two and brought them over to the bed and sat down beside her. Then she asked them again whether the light was alright and they said it was fine. And as soon as they said that she had sat bolt upright in bed, looking past them, and out of her eyes everything that she had ever seen had begun to flow in two almost identical films that ran down her face and over the bed and onto the floor and out the door, while they sat and watched and everything became clearer and clearer.

The Eight Cakes

AT A GIVEN moment in your life eight cakes are being eaten.

The first is in the very country you are in. It is a blood-colored cupcake. It is being raised from a box, on a train, by someone who is used, at last, to your absence.

The second is in another country. It is stone-colored, but iced with nuts and cherries. It is being eaten in the dining room small as an infant greenhouse, though the meals in that family are taken in the unlit kitchen. Plants are standing everywhere, veiling the huge old radio and the piles of magazines. The cake is the first admission of pleasure in that house after the most recent of many deaths. You too have eaten cake from that table but you will not sit down in that room again.

The third is in a third country. It is pale yellow. It is stale. The mice are eating it, in the light of dawn, far above the wide silent water, while in the next room someone long close to you dreams again and again that you are lost.

The fourth is white. Two pieces of it are sitting on a marble table in a crowded tea-room and have not yet been touched by two greedy old ladies, both of whom you have known, who have not seen each other for years. Neither of them will give you a thought. Why should they?

The fifth is in the same country as the second. It is green. It is being eaten by an official whose face you cannot see. He is wearing a flat tie-clasp and no jacket over his nylon shirt. Beside the plate on his desk are documents relating unfavorably to you. He does not like the cake.

The sixth is chocolate. It is being eaten by a child sitting in a chair in which you learned the meaning of "venereal." But the child and you will never meet, and the chair, like the Bourbons, learned nothing.

The seventh is pink. You are eating it yourself out of politeness and boredom, among people who have provided it themselves and whom you will almost certainly never see again.

The eighth is dark purple. The hand that is cutting it drops the knife, and the hand's owner then thinks of you.

Humble Beginning

WHEN he had learned how to kill his brother with a rock he learned how to use a rock to begin stairs. For both of which secrets he thanked the rock.

He considered the rock further. It had always been there keeping secret what it could do. It had never so much as hinted at what it had already done. Now it was keeping all of its other secrets. He fell on his knees facing it and touched it with his forehead, his eyes, his nose, his lips, his tongue, his ears.

He thought the rock had created him. He thought that.

The Smell of Cold Soup

You know at once that it is leaking in from some other part of your life to which your eyes, and indeed all your other senses, are closed. Is it from some sector or plane that you have forgotten? Is it, in that case, from somewhere that you have been? Or from somewhere that you have not been? And if you have not been there, why not? Out of neglect? If so, how dim and gloomy it must be there by now. Smell. The abandoned cobwebs sagging with dust and grease, stretching as far as you can see in every direction. Their dead weavers rocking among them. The cold is not the cold of winter, which contains the promise of spring.

This invisible cold soup is what is fed to the invisible prisoners. It is perfectly nourishing. They do not die in the present. They are dying elsewhere. But they would do that, after all, whatever they were fed.

Gray waves shiver through the cobwebs. It is the war. Even now attempts are being made to improve the lot of the prisoners. Far out of sight a bird, a large unidentified bird, tries to bring them news, tacking and wheeling among the webs, but he is caught and hangs with his neck broken. Yet they must not despair. It may have been a false bird, with false messages. From the same direction someone is running toward them, a tiny figure, waving, shouting, but nothing can be heard. Always one can tell that one of the senses has been shut off. Is it the only one?

Would the news mean anything to them by now?

One should not allow such a question to cross one's mind (a false bird again). You know from the smell of cold soup that they would still understand if you were to break through to them—as you could if you really cared enough—and tell them that whatever else happens we have not ceased to be ourselves, and that the war is still going on somewhere.

The Cheese Seller

EVERYTHING, they say, everything that ever exists even for a moment floats on the black lake, the black lake, and there at each moment what is reflected is its opposite what is reflected is. This is one of the basic truths, without which existence itself would be impossible. How can that be? Opposite in what respect? In one single aspect of the thing? If the thing is upright, for instance, the reflection is upside-down. Yes, that, I say, I can see. In two aspects? If the thing is moving from its right to its left, the reflection is moving from its left to its right. I say I can follow that too. In three aspects? If the thing is black the reflection is white. Alright, I say, I can go that far (though I have a moment of wondering "What if the thing had been blue?" And I could get lost there, because I never was much good at the more abstract forms of mathematics.) If the thing is only a few years from its birth then the reflection, presumably, is only a few years from its death. Well, I say, but there must come a point at which just one too many aspects of a thing are reflected as their opposites, after which the reflection is no longer recognizable, seems to bear no conceivable relation to the thing. Why must such a point come? they ask. Because I cannot imagine it otherwise, I answer. That, they say, is why the lake is black.

And so somewhere on that dark surface is the cheese seller's opposite, the opposite of that moment a long time ago, and my opposite in it. And so instead of coming from the hospital, as we were doing, probably we are going to the hospital. We? Leave that out of it. Instead of there being someone there—no, I will keep to the cheese seller's place itself, the lake is black enough. If I was a child—no, I will leave myself out of it for the moment, if I can. Except that this time I am permitted to stay and listen to him, I am allowed to go with him (do I recognize him, do I recognize anything, do I know where I am?) through the upside-down door. We make our way up, walking on the ceiling. His voice must be the same, aha! Or is only its opposite to be heard echoing over the black surface? Well, I must assume that I know it. That my opposite knows it. And there we are, I am listening to the opposite of the interrupted discourse—the uninterrupted discourse. Instead of lamenting the gradual disappearance of the no-longer appreciated cheeses out of the past, on each of which he once laid an affectionate hand, he is extolling the sudden emergence of the highly-esteemed cheeses of the future, which are ranged around him on plates, from each of which his hand rises in turn like the cover of a chafing dish, to show that the plate is empty. Instead of my heart being variously oppressed by my heart being variously oppressed by the interruption, by not being allowed to listen, the interruption, by not being allowed to listen, by the neglect of the old cheeses one by one, it is variously delighted by the untroubled encomium, the prospect of—no, I will go on leaving myself out of it.

Well, you cannot do that forever, they say. You remember that the cheese seller himself is in the past.

Far in the past, I say, wondering why the recollection ever attracted me.

Therefore his opposite, they say, his opposite—

So I will come to him one day, I suppose. No, I say, it is only my opposite who will come to him. And will find him easily, it must be, in the midst of a time of untroubled happiness, and will share without misgivings his innocent pleasure in the ethereal delicacies of tomorrow. And later even the hospital room will be empty.

At this they say nothing. They are not even there. All by myself I remember the color of the lake which I cannot see.

A Lost Tribe

I T HAS no name. Too many tribes have been lost and
there are not enough names as it is. And in the days
when names were lent to them the lost tribes never gave
them back. The names were never heard of again. They
have been lost as well. Somewhere the lost tribes unpack
them when they halt to make camp in the evening, and
later turn them over beside the fire, when they have
eaten, and by the dying light ponder these now almost
meaningless relics of an abandoned life. They put them
away before they sleep. Worn smooth.

They have left us to die alone. They have left us the
whole world to die in, alone. They have left each one of
us. Some did not even wait until we were born. We did
not even have a chance to watch them go. We did not
even have a chance to say, "Go in peace" (for we would
have said that) "and we will take care of your things
until the day we die." What things? They left none.
And what good would it have done to mention death?
A thing which does not effect them. A place they will
not know.

From each of us they have set out. Each of us has lost
and lost, and the tribes, when we looked, had gone.

There is no tracing them. They would be harder to follow than those war parties of the Tewas who shod themselves with discs so that pursuers would not know whether they had been coming or going, or than their neighbors whose tracks were erased by friendly ants. These tribes have neither enemies nor friends. And still they leave us. Whenever we have chosen, they were the other. There is no way of calling to them.

We have clung to promises. They have marched through the Promised Land again and again and not recognized it.

This evening one of the nameless ones, one of mine, I think, has come down through a pass in the ice somewhere. Oh their hymns of arrival, which I can never hear! Before them is an empty lake surrounded by snow. They eat in haste, then the fires are made to blaze up and once more they start to tell the story, beginning with the ancestor, a shadow who came to a fork. At last they sleep. Tomorrow the snow will be unmarked. Tomorrow night they will not tell of this place. They will repeat the old story about a path, a story which by now is their home, and which they believe.

The Camel Moth

THERE is a moth so small that it can walk through the eye of any needle and look up at the arch overhead as at the ceiling of an enormous gateway. In this world it lives on the fur of camels. It burrows into the hair at the roots and lays its eggs. The larvae dig deeper into the roots and devour them, and from this nourishment each of them spins a length of thread, fastens one end to itself, passes the other end to a neighbor, and then falls asleep. In due course the hairs drop out and blow away over the desert, bearing with them the dormant banqueters. These can survive in a state of suspended animation for centuries, for millenia, for at least as long as the hair of a camel, in the desert climate, can resist the blandishments of decay. When a hair beaches at last on some appropriate shore the sleepers wake and emerge from the minute opening at their end. They come out very slowly, in single file, linked to each other by the silken strand which they had woven before they fell asleep. They are blind. They come forth in silence, a colorless caravan, bearing their colorless thread, as though through the eye of a needle. They enter the earth or any solid object on its surface and stitch their way into it farther and farther.

The fabric of their unseen journeys holds the visible world together. And they move on slowly, searching, searching, until the odor of camel hatches them out all together, with eyes open on their heads, and eyes on their wings, and they fly off to their next living mountain.

They have existed far longer than their hosts. In the aeons before camels came into being this same race of moths lived on other species that have vanished without a trace.

And even these moths are part of the kingdom and numbered among its servants. But a great while before they wake in heaven where there is no devouring and no change, the camels themselves will have vanished from this world and its riches, and will have emerged in the living tapestry of paradise, naked as their tongues.

Among Mutes

EVEN things divulge the form of their desires, if we
could read their lips. Everything that is reflected
in a window or a polished surface is being judged for its
likeness to a glacier. Which may never have existed.

It is one of the many unacknowledged gifts of Hermes, the God of Delusion, to those images imprisoned behind their own eyes, men. He had to deal with them. He got to know them, in the manner of dealers. He watched them dragging their shadows in ignorance—those bonesless black banners that were all that was left of their wings. He watched their blood groping through their brains like the ghost of an amputated limb, looking for the sea. He was moved—not by pity, of course, to which he is eternally immune, but by an impulse to elicit from mortals a fuller admiration of his own command of distance, his grasp of the elements, his ability to transmit himself instantly from world to world. He was moved by vanity, of which he is one of the lavish princes. And by his own love of idleness—he thought he might make his missions easier, by making his activity more apparently comprehensible.

He gave men the idea of travel.

Before that they had simply travelled, transporting their limbs, just as they were, from place to place in answer to specific needs as they recognized them. Men moved heavily, in comparison with many of their forbears, or with him, for example, but they were going through an awkward phase. They were changing. Something which he did not take into account, but no matter—what is done is done. He gave them the idea of travel. Or rather he fished it out of their dreams and presented it to them like a new life, which in a way it is.

And it may be said that few men have ever travelled since. Not in the old manner, slow but honest. Slow but whole. The irrevocable gift worked its way between men's minds and their journeys, widening the split. From then on even the possibility of actual simple travel receded into the past, and men staggered and sank under the influences of a new freedom balanced by a new slavery. Now they could envisage travelling—that was the freedom. They could sit or lie still, at home, and watch the ports fall astern, the waves part, the clouds slip from them; they could hear the shouting in outlandish market-places, and attend while the exotic streamed forward bowing to each of their senses. And they could summon in luminous detail the remotest places in which they had found themselves in the past. They could revisit them again and again. They could establish a living contact with them. They could evolve a conception of a coherent world in every part of which they could move freely. In their minds.

But by contrast what they referred to now as travel was a poor paralyzed state. Energetic vehicles containing their mortal limbs continued, it is true, to depart and arrive, reaching farther, providing greater comfort, assuring greater safety, realizing greater speed. But it became evident that all they were doing was killing distance, killing time, turning the one into the other and removing the corpses of both. Often the bodies of men were not even carried from one genuine place to another genuine place, but were merely hauled past the bodies of other men, between interchangeable settings. Meanwhile the individuals being transported saw an arrangement of objects moving, but they sat still. Everything that was rushing past them was outside them. Cut off from them, and cutting itself off from them farther and farther. It was displaying its unreality to the travellers, who were not there where it was, but inside themselves, sitting still, looking out. They could not touch what was passing— their "travel." Only rarely and confusedly could they be touched by it, by fragments of it, and often what they chose to mistake, in the poverty of the moment, for actual travel, was merely their sedentary contact with other travellers, strangers passing through a synchronous remoteness and absence. Almost the only occasions that from time to time restored reality to travel were those in which it was suddenly invaded by "accident"—by disaster, which is presided over by gods even greater than Hermes.

But once the travellers arrived, once they had again acquiesced to their unchanging circumstance, and had sat down in some room or other that would never move except to fall, then travel, the habitual figment, could embrace even those meaningless itineraries which they had just exhausted. And the solid walls around them, the local air, could be made to yield up all the experiences which the travellers might have had on their vacant journeys, and which in fact they may really have glimpsed, but not tasted, not believed, not made theirs, as they passed. Or those same soon-familiar walls might remove themselves entirely, making way once more for the unsubstantial places where the travellers now might be.

But the wish on which the travel figment was fed never forsook them. It was a wish that, in its true form, no god would have understood. If only, it kept saying, we could set out now, just as we are, and leave ourselves.

The Baptist's Singers

EACH time the varnish of the carriage fills me with a profound but unexpected delight such as rises from the sudden recollection of something loved in child-hood and long forgotten. The luster of the varnish is so deep that it appears to have its own source of light, which moves under the surface, approaches, fades, di-vides and comes together and disappears according to a pleasure of its own. The motions of the light bear wit-ness to something in the nature of the carriage, and to some appearances of the world that it passes, but how-ever closely they are watched, their play looks as though it were independent of both. And I realize each time, when it is too late, that the motions of the light in the varnish have so captivated me that I cannot say with any certainty what color the varnish is. I know it is dark. Some opalescent shade scarcely distinguished from black. But not black. And on the side of the carriage, in an arc like a rainbow's, are the words THE SINGERS, in blue letters edged with little flames of green and gold, and under them is a painting of John the Baptist standing thigh-deep in the sky-blue Jordan.

The horses are dark too, but not black, and their wine-red harness, and the carriage itself, stream with white ribbons tied in little bows.

In the carriage the four singers face each other: two women, one young and pale, the other with a darker complexion and heavy features, both of them in the wide bonnets of another time, both of them in long gloves, with which they hold their stringed instruments. They are riding backwards. Across from them a portly man in a tall hat and a ginger coat, and a boy in black velvet, are sitting, the boy holding a flute. All four of them appear to be laughing merrily at their own conversation. Their heads nod, but nothing can be heard.

The footman raises the long coach horn but if he blows it I cannot hear it. The coachman in his dark coat drives on, slowly, and the carriage moves on as smoothly as a barge. The blue wheels turn on the glassy surface of the road, where rain has just fallen. The carriage glides along on its reflection, the blue wheels spinning above and below, making no mark where they touch, and then very slowly the wheels begin to sink into their reflections. The rims disappear. The wheels above and below share a lost segment that grows like the rising of an invisible sun. And now the footman is surely blowing his long gleaming horn, but there is not a sound to be heard as the carriage sinks into itself, and the feet of John the Baptist meet, stand on each other, and are washed away, and the Jordan is swallowed up in the Jordan, and the singers in the singers. Only a piercing silence rises from both coach horns, and continues to echo long after they themselves are out of sight.

The Roofs

THERE are woods close to our village. Thin at the edges, but you cannot see far into them. They are broken here and there by tracts of empty plain that stretch all the way to the horizon. The birds that approach and recede above the dark woods are not the same as those that rise and dip over the treeless spaces between. The birds of the woods reflect darkness. Those of the open ground flash like signals of light. It is beyond these signals, across one of the tracts of open country, to the east, that the roofs of the other village can be seen above the horizon. Only the roofs—the steeples, the peaks of gables, the smoke from chimneys. When the sun sets on our village the roofs of the other are already a part of night.

No messages come from there. None are sent there. No one from our village ever went there, or would admit to having gone. The very subject is frowned upon, and the elders answer all questions about the other village with an abrupt and unyielding silence. But it is only the very young children who ever ask such questions, and they seldom persist beyond the second or the third time. Then they begin to wonder whether the roofs on the horizon are not something which only they see. As for the idea of going to the other village, by the time we can walk any such notion seems as remote from possibility as does that of flying by flapping our arms.

But I dreamed of the other village. It was a dream that returned at intervals over several years, always essentially the same, but always in greater detail. Gradually I came to know the other village in those dreams: the corners of lanes, the massive stone portals, the doors open into courtyards, the smells of cow barns and of meals cooking over fires fed with some unfamiliar wood, the backs of women vanishing into kitchen doors, leaving their fresh-hung laundry behind them—it's true I never saw their faces. And I never heard anything as I walked through the winding streets which at last joined each other like sections of a jig-saw puzzle, forming an image through which I could find my way from one place to another, with no blanks at all. But only outside: I never saw the interiors of the houses, except for an occasional glimpse through an open window of a fly on an empty table, or a plate standing on edge. Still, the image was as complete as any map, and once that was so I began to be possessed by a wish to visit the other village. I knew I could tell no one of this desire, and the sense of the folly of such a wish grew with the wish itself, but could not prevent it or even diminish it. I was appalled to find that I was beginning to lay plans.

There are no roads over the plain between our village and the other. And even if there were, how could I have set out to walk there in full view of my neighbors? I would have to take one of the paths into the woods, and then turn aside once I was out of sight, hoping that I would not lose my bearings. I would go in the morning, when every man in the village left for the day's work on some piece of land or other that belonged to him. I would leave earlier than the others so that I would not have to lie. I would carry an axe as though I were going to cut wood. As others would be doing, for it was August.

And from the path I turned north and made my way to the edge of the woods, where I could see both our village and the roofs of the other, and I started toward the roofs, keeping among the trees. I soon realized that the other village was much farther than I had grown to believe. I crossed broad hollows from which even the steeple was not visible. The sun was almost at the zenith when I came to the top of a gradual rise and saw in front of me, close at hand, the steeple, the gabled roofs, the smoking chimneys, down as far as I had always seen them, and below that point nothing. Air. The plain, going on, with birds flashing across it, in silence. The roofs did not even cast shadows on the ground.

It may be that I should have turned back then. But I walked on, down the long slope, and took my first step among the roofs. And my second. Looking up. I recognized where I was, from the dreams, though the walls of the first storeys, the doorways, the windows were not there, and I was walking on the unmarked plain. I passed the steeple. I looked up into its darkness and saw long ropes emerging from the black and then dissolving at the same height at which everything else dissolved, but swaying as though they ended far below. I reached out to see if I could feel a wall where I could see none; I walked on, that way, groping in the daylight, but I could feel nothing. In the dormer window of one of the largest houses I saw a face, in the shadow of a shawl, watching me. It turned away at once and I saw the shawl descending stairs, and then reappearing at another window, turning again, going down more stairs, coming —as I thought—to meet me. But the stairs never emerged below the horizon line, and I stood watching the empty windows. I wanted to call. What could I call? I waited a long time. Then I turned back. At the line of trees I looked around and the horizon had risen again to support the roofs.

But now it's my own village that eludes me. Suddenly I look up and above a certain line I see nothing but air, and through it, far away, the birds of the woods. Members of my own family climb stairs and vanish, head-first, step by step, and I want to call, but what could I call? And night after night I am still staring up into darkness when the sun, no doubt, is already playing among the doors of the other village.

The Abyss

O<small>N</small> <small>OCCASIONS</small> whose return—more and more frequent—obeys some law that I perceive only dimly, if at all, I open my eyes, and instead of the world where the days have names and belong to weeks, I see that I am really still hanging by my breath, high in space, with night already advanced and no prospect of a morning.

Here I am, tilted far forward as though I were swimming, yet I dare not risk a swimmer's gestures to his element. I hardly dare move at all. I ease my breath out, I draw it back cautiously. The slightest jar would dislodge me from here, where I am suspended. Then I would drop through the darkness as though a hand had let me go. For I am held up by nothing but a transparent film like the skin of a bubble, which stretches across the darkness from side to side. Above it my head. Below it everything else. It fits close around my breath, as long as I breathe in and out very slowly so as not to break the seal. And I am trying to move forward.

Below me, far below me, the light is a little clearer, but it is sealed away from my eyes, and only in that condition can it shine. After all, it is the same way with the filaments in bulbs. Below me a faint glow, made possible by the membrane in which I am hanging, cautiously looking down. There is a house I know, I am sure, there by the river like a line of paint, the vein of the valley. There's the little path behind it, climbing the ridge. I remember how it twists its way into the first high village, and arrives at the fountain. I must not follow it. I must not be drawn down from my breath. If the seal breaks, the bubble will vanish, and the lights will go out below as I begin to fall.

The film in which I am trying to move forward may be stretched from the horizons, but I cannot see that far. I catch reflections, at moments, from its surface, but whether from the upper or the lower side I cannot tell. It seems to be waving up and down very slowly, like sea swells in a calm, or like another breath. I see my body just beneath the film, like the limbs of a doll twin in a toy bath tub, there under the transparent surface. What can I do? I long to move forward. But I dare not reach out or grasp—there is nothing to grasp. I dare not call. Who would I call? Silently, watching the shadowy valley rise and sink below me, I say to my breath once again, little breath come from in front of me, go away behind me, row me quietly now, as far as you can, for I am an abyss that I am trying to cross.

Knives

AROUND us hangs a curtain like rain. Around us, spirits of salt waiting for our griefs to release us. We cannot touch the curtain. It hangs in front of the days and nights, the sun and the earth. It wears us away but we believe we would be nothing without it. Or if not nothing, then naked. Our spirits scarcely speak. Could they pass through the curtain without us? Have we no others? We look out and see nothing, through the curtain, but uses.

We look at the knives, those gentle creatures, many of them older than we are. We see only the service we ask of them—separation, separation, and pain. Without which, as we say, we would be nothing. So we never see those meek faces themselves, moving in a world upon which they open no eyes at all, about which they know nothing, and of whose savageries they have become a symbol. They who eat nothing, who do not even defend themselves against the dew, against rust, against any of the bearers of loss, and who make no sound, except an occasional clear note like the calling of a bird, when they have been struck, or abraded with a stone. They who will obey any guide.

Knives

Through the curtain we look at them shining quietly on the wall and we are nudged by a vision of a bloody shore.

The Hours of a Bridge

WHEN the black.
When the lamps fill, when the lamps empty.
When a prayer. With no one praying it. Oh yes there
is someone but they are hanging back, hanging back. All
through the darkness. In the daytime they are nothing
but a long gasp. When a prayer they let the prayer go
ahead by itself and they hang back and become deserted.

When a prayer again. No shoes running after it with a
limp. Or is that the prayer? No stars. Above or below.
And still long long before.

When a rat. When a flag. A long flag.

When the battle will cross. But that will be by its own
light. Between the smug statues.

When the sins of the night, in a butcher's cart. The
same cart that is used for the plagues. A dog painted on
the side. A dog walking under it. Mist walking on each
side. The wheels and the cart and the dogs and the mist
and the sins all unaware of each other.

When the man with the red hood that looks black.
Going home.

When the battle will cross again, coming back. When
the statues will all become statues of the death of the air.

When the dawn's cat. Sits right down. By a coat, getting light.

When the coat is disturbed water runs out of it. Old water. Old old water.

But the best thing for us, we believe, is to go on for as long as we can, living upstream, tending our instruments by night. On the one bank.

Tracks

O SUMMER-FACED patience, how long you have
waited, and nothing must have seemed certain.
But I know at last. I see that we will come after all, you
and I, to a white house at the top of a long street. It sits
there waiting for us, empty. Every morning the yellow
sunlight streams in through the windows which face out
on the other side, away from the street that climbs the
hill, just as it will stream in on the morning when we will
be shown into the house, through the bright airy rooms,
with my mother patting the cushions, opening the big
cupboards, my father fingering the cord of a blind at a
shining window, everyone brimming with recent knowledge, with revelation, with arrival, with peace. The house
stands in a row with several others along the top of the
hill. It is quiet up there: no traffic, no sounds from
the other houses when the windows are opened and the
spring air flows in. On the other side of the house—the
front—the railroad track runs past the door, as in so
many of the towns through which the history of my
family has been threaded. But here the track—a single
line—gives off silence. It is beginning to rust, even
though it is almost new. Grass is starting to grow be-

tween the ties. Beyond the track the cliff falls away abruptly. It is a sheer drop of several hundred feet, and at the bottom the details of the landscape emerge only partially, here and there, from the gray mist.

In front of the porch, in the middle of the tracks, an upright stake of angle-iron is fixed into the crushed rock of the roadbed; it is painted black and yellow; other stakes of the same kind can be seen at intervals, every few ties, for some fifty feet in either direction. The tracks are not to be used. No trains will pass the house, making it tremble. My father will lead me—as he has never done—across the tracks themselves, as though they belonged to the family at last. He will point to the bends in either direction and explain that although trains might conceivably come that far still, they would not continue. Just the same, he will show me the source of his worry: the place almost across from the house, where the tracks ran until recently when the top of the cliff gave way under a coal train and the locomotive and the cars poured like an iron waterfall onto the misty rocks far below. It will seem, as he tells it, as though echoes of the crash were still rising from the gray valley. The new tracks have been set farther back from the edge, and blocked with painted spikes on which the paint is kept fresh, and my father knows and approves of the man in charge, and for the time being no trains will come past the bends, but my father's worry will not sleep. In a low voice, so that no one else will hear, in a few words, he will let me know his fear that the edge of the cliff will continue to collapse. At some hour when we do not expect it the new tracks will sag and snap and swing down over nothing, as though through water, groping, and the house will plunge after them, shrieking and ripping, into the gray abyss. He will inform me that none of the houses on either side is lived in at present.

But I will laugh and say that his fears are exaggerated,

that what the place needs is to have us living in it, us, .
with what we know now, with the sunlight and its welcome, with the sense that the house is ours and has been
waiting for us, and that no evil can befall us there. I will
tell him all that, quietly, calmly, smiling, as to a child,
and without believing a word I say.

Memorials

ONE AFTER the other, if they are not wholly lost, our intentions, unless they started that way, turn into legends. On the other side of their effects we walk on, thinking we know. And they, whom we continue to address and refer to as though their presence were something that we understood perfectly and could take for granted, leave us without our so much as noticing. Yes, sometimes most of them will be gone at a time, while our activities continue without them. And then they will return across great distances, like the influences of planets, and even when they are reborn in something very like the old forms it is probable that we will not recognize them, any more than we did the last time. It is this aspect of existence that—without our meaning it—our monuments commemorate.

After each war the men from the memorial companies tour the little towns. On their arrival the custodians of the locally accepted intentions welcome them. These neighborhood officials, thoroughly rehearsed, impress themselves once again, in a manner that has acquired its own rough ritual, with the superstitions that they now believe were the intentions (including their own) underlying the recent conflict, and with the feelings which, in consequence, they had encouraged themselves to profess. They are scrupulously mindful of what they take to be the intentions of their neighbors, hereby to be commemorated—the grief of widows and bereaved mothers, the proud and vengeful wrath of fathers, the as yet undeveloped but indubitable gratitude of children. Insofar as their combined means will allow—and this is not something over which any of them would wish to be sparing, or would admit to such a wish if he felt it—they want an object that will express all of these things clearly, changelessly, and in perpetuity. In this spirit they approach the latest catalogues.

Also they have piously in mind what they take to have been the intentions of the young men who went away and died. Quite as much—more so—than the actual features of their faces (though they have not ruled out a hope, of course, of finding a happy resemblance, and with this in view, rather than trust their pathetic memories they come provided with photographs collected from the bereaved but supposedly proud households). Furthermore, the intentions with which these youths are presumed to have faced the fatal conflict, or confronted death itself when it stood before them, must also be represented. The catalogues are limited, naturally, and such individual matters are now beyond verification. Something at last is chosen which is felt to be, within the practical limitations, suitably sad and suitably noble, to commemorate all of these fictions.

And the result, for heaven knows how many years afterwards, graces the little square in all weathers, with the names on its base and the war in which they were called meaning less and less to more and more people. Familiarity and the symmetry of its surroundings before long set about making the object itself grow dim. What it evokes, in a while, to many of those who see it, both natives and strangers, is the boredom of the square, the elusiveness of meaning, the anonymity in which the names, even of the living, are ghosts, the delusions of others, at times even a shifty levity, and at times an uncomprehended and unmentioned fear.

I N A RICH provincial city there is a museum as impos-
ing and quite as large as any in the capital. The façade is immense and the portico dwarfs the visitor,
seeming to fill the space between his usual size and his
shrunken self with an echo. The style of the building is
not obviously contemporary, though it could have been
produced by no other age. It manages to suggest, with its
general proportions, high columned halls, and open airy
courts surrounded by enormous arcades, an entire classical tradition in which temple and palace are never completely distinguishable from each other. The approach
to the building is lined on either side with marble pedestals, each of them empty. Across the top of the main portal there is a large panel for a name or inscription. It is
blank.

The museum is referred to, in the literature supplied
by the chamber of commerce, as The Permanent Collec-
tion—the gift of an anonymous donor. The terms of the
donor's will stipulated that there should be no other des-
ignation. But publications for which the city administra-
tion cannot be held accountable reveal that the museum
was the bequest of a local millionaire whose forbears,

through several generations, had played a dominant role in the exploitation of that region. The name is common in those parts, on streets, banks, office buildings, bridges, housing developments, foundations. But the family—at least the direct line for which these have all been named —has died out. The last of the line was the builder and donor of the museum.

In his youth, according to the local historians, he had fallen in love with the daughter of another wealthy household, at a northern resort where both dynasties had summer houses. Only one portrait of her is known to have survived. It shows the girl at the time when they first met—already beautiful: slender, dark-haired, her expression gentle, delicate, remote. She had pretended not to notice his early, clumsy suit. During the first winters her name was coupled with one boy after another from the same schools which he attended. But one summer, perhaps out of mere indolence, she had paid him more attention, or at least had spent more time in his company than before, and their families had come to take the relation between them for granted—though neither of the young people did so. They were spoken of for a winter or so almost as though they were engaged. Between the assumption, which he met on all hands, of his future with her, and the secret barrenness of his hopes, he became aware of an abyss that would swallow everything he knew.

During college he had seen as much as possible of a succession of other girls. He had even formed attachments with several of them, lasting for a matter of months. But she was the one whom he tried not to want, and the longing for her grew with him. He proposed to her before he left college and she listened to him quietly and told him she wanted to wait. Then she had gone abroad with her family and he was not surprised when, shortly after their return, he received an announcement of her engagement to someone else.

They had continued to see each other, occasionally. She had had a daughter. He too had married—twice, once hilariously, both times disastrously. He had had no children.

Her marriage too had ended in divorce, after fifteen years. Her husband spent his summers on his own estate, and her daughter was sent to be with him in June. She herself had returned to visit her family, in the northern resort. There she had seen her former suitor again. There had been a second courtship, to which he deliberately imparted an air of casual urbanity that was as contrived —on his part—as the stillness of the breath above a trigger-finger. It worked. They were married during the following winter. Nothing is known of their life together. Outwardly it was placid. She died a year later, while swimming.

The entrance to the museum is guarded by wardens in plain dark uniforms without metal buttons or insignia of any kind. Inside the main portal is a vast hall, with another marble pedestal in the center, catching the light. It is empty, like those outside. In the walls on either side are tall niches, also containing nothing. Guards in the same featureless uniforms stand in pairs at each doorway, and at intervals along the corridors and in the arcades. There is a prescribed order for visiting the rooms, and the guards point the way.

And in each room there are more of the large pedestals, without statues or names. In some, besides, there are glass display cases, of different shapes and sizes, empty, and picture frames containing blank canvas on the walls. All along the arcades there are empty niches and pedestals, alternating, and in each of the courtyards there is an empty fountain. No one talks. It takes well over an hour to make the tour of the rooms and step out into the world again on the same side as the entrance but farther along.

From there one leaves by another walk flanked by empty pedestals. The donor lived to see the building completed, but the public was admitted only after his death.

Why did he want the visitors at all? Could he have forseen those who come out from the building with a sigh of relief and a joke, or with a burst of indignation at the abuse of wealth or at the enormity of his egoism or with a yawn, a glance at a watch, a suggestion about eating? Could he have forseen those who emerge from time to time in silence, with their faces shining?

The June Couple

I F WE could afford it, he says, we have often said that
we would have a little place beside the water. He
enjoys saying *little place* even more than *beside the water*. *Beside the water* comes to him like an old pleasure
which is becoming increasingly a matter of memory.
The water is forever darkening. It always seems farther
away. By now it might be dark glass. With artificial
reeds growing through it, and life-like ducks among
them. But *little place* announces his firm hold on the
world of men, and his aspirations in it, even those he
would not otherwise admit to.

Yes, she says, we've imagined from the beginning how
we'd love to have a place of our own somewhere by the
water. When she says *from the beginning* she can actually feel the air near the water, and the water itself,
which is only slightly cooler, and moving slowly, a quiet
stream passing through a meadow under old trees.

One day maybe we'll take a house by a lake, he says.
One day maybe. Take a small house. By the age at which
he imagined such a thing might be possible he would
phrase the suggestion with a wink.

She sighs and says, it was one of the first things we

realized we agreed about. We love to imagine standing watching the water flow quietly by.

Needn't be anything elaborate, he says. A simple cottage, after all. Envisaging a lake-side construction covered with tan imitation-brick shingle, with a screened porch all along each end.

It's all I ever want, she says. Her eye filling, as so often, with a picture of a low stone building, one tiny dormer in its thatch roof open toward the breathing sounds of the trees over the stream. And there they both stand, between the door and the water, on the soft grass, with a family of ducks threading past them, and her cat at her feet. Her husband is wearing a top hat and a white dress uniform with gold frogs and she is most becomingly dressed as a shepherdess. Both of them in Sevres.

He sees them standing outside the screen-porch to be photographed.

No one is watching. Her parents are out. She puts her tongue (as she has been strictly forbidden to do) to both of the figures. It is just as she had imagined. Sugar. Like all secrets. The cottage is sugar too, and the pink and white clouds. And at the edge of the sky, beyond the little crooked fence, there is a round window with little roses all around it, and an eye filling the whole window.

Yes, he says, looking out over the first few feet of still water, at the black camera occupying the middle foreground, with the sun on its shoulder. He has recognized the eye filling the whole of the lens.

Yes, he says proudly. Mine.

Yes, she sighs, in utter agreement, recognizing the eye filling the window at the end of the sugar sky. Mine.

The Wives of the Shipbreakers

No. The wives of the new shipbreakers. The distinction must be made at once, and they help to make it. They do more than help. Properly observed, they would be enough by themselves to make the distinction clear. To make it clear, first, and in a short time to make it seem inevitable. Is this surprising, after all? It certainly does not surprise everyone. There were cool heads that foresaw it in the earliest stages of the planning, and among them were those who urged most insistently that the new shipbreakers should remain celibate. But irony triumphed, and they were overruled on the ill-defined grounds of humanity.

It might almost be said that the distinction, in some sense, is made clear only by the wives of the new shipbreakers. The new shipbreakers themselves, after all, are never seen by the world at large. It is scarcely just to reproach their wives for keeping together, as they tend to do. Yet some people naturally resent any such behavior in others, since it bespeaks a secret—something in the order of a different language, sometimes a pain from which those who watch are excluded. And everything from which they are excluded and to which others cling they suspect of being a privilege, a real one, which reminds them that their own (which they praise and defend, therefore, with new fierceness) are substitutes.

It may be that the wives of the new shipbreakers do, in fact, keep tgether more exclusively than is necessary. But how can we judge? What do we know of their reasons, of the persistency and discomfort of their need on the one hand to remain apart from all who do not share the peculiar knowledge and questions of their existence, and on the other to seek what reassurance may be found in the company of those who may be called their colleagues? Some of their neighbors even find grounds for resentment in the fact that all of the wives of the new shipbreakers maybe presumed to be in their present condition voluntarily. A few of them married new shipbreakers after the men had decided to enter upon that irrevocable calling. Others had been free (as the neighbors put it) to leave their husbands, if they could not dissuade them, when the men first suggested such employment. It is interesting that very few observers imagine that the extra pay, in itself, could provide the incentive for either the husbands or the wives to embrace such a decision.

It is already possible to recognize one of the wives when she is alone on the street. The complexion, for one thing. No worse, perhaps, than that of many of her compatriots. But as though it had already abandoned the wish to remain skin. A glimpse of earth under artificial light. Then the jaundiced eyes. The teeth, thinning, appearing translucent, flaking. The nails, easily chipped and split. A slackness in the thin legs. Without exception the wives smoke heavily. Pregnancy is rare and so far has miscarried in every instance, though in theory there is no reason why childbirth should not be possible. It is too early to tell—or to predict the effects on any eventual offspring.

The Wives of the Shipbreakers

Remember that the vocation of the new shipbreakers is not surrounded with honor. Rather, their practice is shrouded, and mention of it slurred over in public. The new shipbreakers themselves are allowed to know only a little about what they are called upon to do. And yet some sleepless attraction, some consuming exhileration or unspeakable contentment, the farthest reflections of which remain an exasperation to many who presumably benefit by it, day by day causes the profession to grow. As it must, while the new ships in increasing numbers continue to return.

From a Mammon Card

Those who work, as they say, for a living, are not to calculate how much they make an hour and then consider what they claim to own, remembering that there was a time when they made less per hour, and then consider that what they claim to own is perhaps all that remains of what they sold that many hours of their life for, and then try to imagine the hours coming again.

The Uncle

Yes, but to fall heir in the middle of some night to this huge blistered edifice with its once-white clapboard here and there swinging loose in the ceaseless wind of the prairie and knocking on the walls like boats. And so to wake one morning in front of a box-shaped facade facing north on the edge of a small town, with a broad level expanse of cinders in front of it where trucks could pull in, where the tracks of a long-disused trolley line still run, where puddles are spread out like a cold day's laundry, and the weeds are moving in. To stand in front of it under its own unrepeatable clouds and to hear the silence coming from the building coming from the building coming from the building as a whole and dwarfing the voices of the local worthies in their darkest suits emerging ahead of you and around you from their dark cars drawn up on the edge of the cinders as on the edge of a beach. The silence coming from the building and drowning the notes of their car doors slamming, of their affable weightless exchanges. The tones of undifferentiated and unexamined respect with which they approach, continuing explanations of a life that is theirs but which they persist in describing as though it were a complex habit which you must surely remember, suddenly, and embrace with joyful tears, and resume. Their behavior is not all of a piece. The manner which they present to you matches the dark clothes and gray faces with rimless spectacles which they have worn for this solemn but singular occasion, but the side of each of them that is turned away from you might well be wearing gaudy sports clothes of some shiny synthetic, which they flash at their clambakes as they spill their beer. It is no surprise that a pair of them, brothers, furniture wholesalers and retailers, prove to be also the leading funeral directors, who had supervised the elaborate ceremonies surrounding the final disposition of your uncle's remains, details of which they keep relaying to you with unfeigned pride as you proceed together across the cinders toward the building. They assure you that nothing that might conceivably have been done had been neglected. That your uncle's wishes, with which they had been thoroughly familiar, had been respected to the letter and indeed far beyond it, far beyond it. That not one of the orders, lodges, fraternities and civic organizations which your uncle had served so selflessly, so unforgettably, and with such distinction in his lifetime (every one of which was represented by some member of the deputation here this morning) had failed to contribute to the memorial services, each with its own most solemn rites and honors and with the presence of all of its most sacred panoplies and paraphernalia, to say nothing of the wreaths. Never in the memory of the town had there been such a show. The attorney and his asistant walk along with the funeral brothers, and the rest take their tone from these.

And in this company to approach the porch running all the way along the front of the building, its gray-painted floor raised only a few inches above the cinders, its high roof sagging just a little between each of the

slender iron uprights topped with its cast pineapple still
bearing the vertical ridges of the mold. To hear the feet,
one by one, step onto the hollow porch, not without a
certain ephemeral reverence despite their familiarity
with the place, and to recognize in that momentary unaccustomed self-consciousness and restraint the influence of the period between that moment and the removal of the uncle's body—an interrum during which
the building had stood alone like a tomb. To notice that
all the windows had been whitened from inside.

Then to watch the attorney step to the door, face the
others, draw from two pockets his black kid gloves, deliberately put them on, smoothing one finger at a time,
draw from a third pocket the will, open it to the relevant
page, re-read the passage relating to the building, the
land around it, and all their contents, then draw from
still another pocket a pair of scissors with which he cuts
the black ribbon stretched across the door from side to
side and sealing it shut. Whereupon his assistant produces
the key to the door and one by one you enter.

To see the enormous center hall with its cobwebbed
ceiling. To glance, in passing, into the dusty wooden
caverns of the flour mill, through a door to the left, and
the corresponding caverns where the sacks were piled,
through a door on the right, and into offices beyond, ob-
serving the shrouded machines and closed roll-top desks
in each. To climb, in that black-suited company, the cobwebbed unpainted stairs with their oft-repaired banis-
ters, and find those who had preceded you drawn up in
front of another ribboned door, named for one of the
local lodges, and to watch the representative of that lodge
take a pair of scissors from his pocket and cut the ribbon
and produce a key and show you a room with some flags
standing in a corner, chairs folded along one wall, and
a paper bell hanging from the light globe. To have that
ritual repeated in room after room of that winding hall,

to a continuo of coughs, shuffling feet, wheezing, whispers, smothered laughs. To be shown a door marked with a sign saying "Ladies," and to see it opened to display a wall covered with pages of ancient fashion magazines and piles of boxes.

To accompany the representatives of the lodges and orders to the top of the stairs and thank each in turn and shake his hand, and return with the attorney and the funeral brothers to a ladder fixed to the wall and climb with them through a trap door to the living quarters above. There to see the immense front bedroom with its shrouded bed the color of dust, its faded green Chinese rug, its massive furniture from the days of the famous blizzards, its gray water-light. The long dining-room, along the east, with its draped table double-ended like a ferry, and its dark ceiling over the china cabinets and the mirrored mantlepiece, on which a black marble clock had stopped promptly at two. To emerge at last in the sanctum itself—the room at the back of the building, facing south, with its wooden ceiling and heavy square table, and its roll-top desk by a dusty window, and its tiers of shelves lined with books and ledgers, and its dirty coffee cup. Here to be given the keys, to be given the papers, to be given all the addresses, to be given all the written instructions, to be shown the safe, to be given the combination, to be shown the little stained bathroom, to be shown the door to the back stairs leading down to the mill and the loading platform and the siding, visible from one window, on which a few empty freight cars are still standing. To notice, instead of listening, the patterned glass of the lamp-shades. To be shown the uncle's diplomas, honors, citations, framed on the walls, and to be left alone at last in that room, looking out of one of the dusty south windows, onto the black-rimmed arm of the lake, the color of steel, in which black barges are sinking all the way to the horizon. A window at which your uncle (on your mother's side) had stood often, imagining the heir who would never know him, who would enter at last, and stand there alone, looking out, thinking of him. It makes you wonder which of you has died.

The Approved

THIS one I was allowed to know. His face was a triangle standing on its point, hiding a parade of hollows. He was allowed to know other schoolfellows. And I was allowed to know him. Sometimes we pretended to a liking which neither of us felt, because it was approved. But no one could walk far on that surface.

He was respectable. At that age. His conduct at school was indeed better than mine, who was allowed to know only him. I with my one-legged japes, ill-timed, the delight of no one, like irrelevant misquotations from a foreign language. Little shames for which I was not otherwise punished because of some undefinable privilege that hedged me around, like a correspondance between a parent and the authorities, which is a great pointer of fingers. But he made no awkward sallies, played the games, was not considered the most cowardly, in fact excelled at catching a ball, and in class answered as well as I did, with the hollows prompting him.

For he too had a source of privilege. It was not his mother alone, who worked all day at a notions counter, suffered with her feet, and heaved herself up on Sundays in the choir to take solo parts in the anthemns, her voice like an empty powder box. She was married to his privilege, she was its daughter as well, and while I knew her she became its mother.

I was allowed to visit their house. He was allowed to go where he pleased and I was allowed to visit him in the dark sagging unpainted building smelling of cats, where the grandmother sat in the kitchen year after year, clutching herself and crying, clinging to the privilege. For they were Death's family. No one contested it. Death visited other dwellings in other streets but that was all in a day's work, and he came back to them to sleep.

Death was the grandmother's father, born in the old country, and she clung to him and showed his picture and told of the food he liked and of how he missed his home. Then Death was the grandmother's husband, also born in the old country, and she showed his picture, so like the other, one man at two different ages, both of them clearly Death, both of them forms of the same presence, the same exaltation. It had brought the old country with it, a weight in a locked trunk on its back, and at night it stretched its legs in the house and the windows rattled and the cats clawed silently at the doors. And Death was the mother's husband, as she had not understood until too late. She never showed his picture. She brought up his two sons and struggled to turn them into repetitions of him. And so it transpired with the elder, who of the two seemed less like him, but who was still a child when he lay in Death's bed like his father and his grandfather and all the other males of the family except the one whom I was allowed to know, and the privilege washed over him like an arm of the sea. In Death's room in which he himself had reverently suspended from the ceiling the paper airplanes which he had made with tireless care. They turned slowly above him—pieces of his memory. In Death's room with its pictures of Death at

all ages, and its lace from the old country, and its gray
wallpaper.

I was allowed to know the youngest because it was a
nice family. And because of the privilege. Sometimes we
imagined that we liked each other, because it was approved. But we never came to trust each other, to laugh,
to be content. He was not Death, but one of Death's
only sons.

A Garden

You are a garden into which a bomb once fell and did not explode, during a war that happened before you can remember. It came down at night. It screamed, but there were so many screams. It was heard, but it was forgotten. It buried itself. It was searched for but it was given up. So much else had been buried alive.

Other bombs fell near it and exploded. You grew older. It slept among the roots of your trees, which fell around it like nets around a fish that supposedly had long since become extinct. In you the rain fell. In your earth the water found the dark egg with its little wings and inquired, but receiving no answer made camp beside it as beside the lightless stones. The ants came to decorate it with their tunnels. In time the grubs slept, leaning against it, and hatched out, hard and iridescent, and climbed away. You grew older, learning from the days and nights.

The tines of forks struck at it from above, and probed, in ignorance. You suffered. You suffer. You renew yourself. Friends gather and are made to feel at home. Babies are left, in their carriages, in your quiet shade. Children play on your grass and lovers lie there in the summer evenings. You grow older, with your seasons. You have become a haven. And one day when a child has been playing in you all afternoon, the pressure of a root or the nose of a mouse or the sleepless hunger of rust will be enough, suddenly, to obliterate all these years of peace, leaving in your place nothing but a crater rapidly filling with time. Then in vain will they look for your reason.

The Bandage

THEY told you, remember, that one day it would come to seem natural. And so it has. You have forgotten their saying it, perhaps, because they were right—the bandage has become so natural to you that you have forgotten its presence. Never notice it. Never realize that your first question, upon waking, is whether it has slipped. Whether it has slipped, you see, not whether it is there. And you know with the lightest of touches whether or not it has slipped, wherever it may be at that moment. You know it even though the bandage wraps a different place every day. That doesn't confuse you. And it doesn't lead you to ponder the shifts of misfortune. No, a slipped bandage is a slipped bandage, wherever it is to be found on waking. It belongs where it is, only more securely.

Yesterday on a leg, today on an ear or an eye—on whatever surface or appendage of your anatomy it is performing its office when you wake, you remember why it is there. And you remember also enough of the accident so that you know you don't want to think of what the bandage mercifully conceals, so that you would never peer under the bandage at the black landscape sunk in its fate. You recall with a lurch of nausea how it happened, what you did wrong. You always think of that when it's too late. Only the bandage, now, can help to make things right—or as right as they can be. Better than before, sometimes, as you know. Whatever the bandage cradles you will have to try to use again as soon as you can, just as you did before. The thought appalls you. The broken, appalled by thoughts of the whole. But every day another part of you reappears, is restored to you again almost as it was, and you never notice. You take it for granted. You forget which limb it was. You grope, delicately, breathlessly, not for the scar, but for the bandage. Where are you? You murmur. How is it with you? And with fingers perfected in humility you tighten it so that you can begin the day.

The Diver's Vision

EVERY season we who have his welfare at heart say again that the champion diver should retire while he is unbeaten. It would be terrible to see someone younger come along and— Though it is impossible to conceive of anyone else approaching him in one respect. At the top of his dive. At the top of his dive he stops. The rest of his diving is superb but is clearly within the province of what flesh and blood can accomplish, given expectional physical gifts and the best training. But at the top of his dive he seems no longer to be one of us. So we honor him. And we hope that we will be able to go on doing so. But each season we are afraid.

The top of his dive seems no less miraculous now that he has explained it. When he reaches that point he looks down. On the water far below him he sees the little slick where he will enter it. A shifting apparition, its edges tattered and melting in a slow film of colorless flames. He waits, hanging in the air, staring down at it, and beholds his own face appear as a veil in the middle of that bit of surface. His own face shifting, tattered and melting, but clearly his, and at moments filled with a blinding radiance that always seems to belong to an instant just past or just about to occur, rather than to the present. Still he waits, and then around the face he catches a glimpse of a perspective which he can never describe afterwards, a landscape leading into other worlds, their love, their silence, the sight of it filling him with a tenderness sudden as lightning, and with a joy that would turn to terror unless he moved at once toward his vision. And so he falls. And as he does it disappears. It fades from his eyes, from his lungs. Not altogether from his memory. Not so completely that he does not know that it will be waiting for him the next time, however the interval is measured.

He will not retire because secretly he wants to go on until the day when he finds in himself the power to hang there at the top of his dive while the terror comes and goes. And then, he believes, the veil of his face will vanish but the vision beyond it will wait for him, clear and unwavering, at least as long as he falls.

The Clover

WELL, I would say at last, when I had come in from
that day's mountain, I will go out now and
mow a little patch of that clover, this evening, for the
beast. And I would take my scythe and sharpen it, with
a sound like the strokes of a dissolving bell. At that hour
the heat would have begun to leave the air. The shadows
would have groped a long way toward the ruined east.
A coolness would be seeping through the stems of the
clover, near the ground at first, but beginning to rise.
The moles would have heard it. The mice would be running through it, small gray teeth from no combs. And
the leaves themselves would be starting to put aside the
gray mask they turn to the sun. They would be rising
like green skies, each stamped with one print of the same
horse, each marked with a single broken orbit, each
mourning a short-lived star. The dew would have just
begun to come home to them from the sky, where it had
been hiding. Well, I would say after a while, I will go
out and cut an armload of that good clover for the beast.

The beast would watch me sharpening the scythe by
the water trough, in whose surface the first lamp was
not yet lit. It would watch me take down from the peg

the folded square of old sacking for carrying home the clover. I would look at the eyes of the beast and see that the night was already there, and I would go out, with the folded sacking on my shoulder and the gray blade glinting.

And there would be the clover, stretching before me, the nation of shadow. I would go along the mossed wall to the stone gate and step through into the field. And step into the secret breathing of the clover, with my scythe. And there, the patch that I had thought to mow, the same, the very patch that I had seen in the late day of my mind—someone would have mown it before me. Someone would have already mown it. The same scythe-shaped segment, the same broken orbit, the same silent smile. Someone else had come and made them. And taken that clover. I would stand there in the little sudden breeze of twilight like a third gate-post. And no one would come. No one would pass. No one would tell me anything.

Evening after evening it would happen and at first I would cut some other place—what I had thought of as some other evenings's clover, or I would take something else back for the beast. To no purpose. What I put in the manger was never touched. I watched the beast carefully, the deep fireless eyes, the nose like a rock out of a waterfall. Nothing seemed wrong. The breath as sweet as ever, the movements as placid, the coat as smooth. The udder as heavy, or heavier. I would pull up the three-legged stool and start milking. At the time I was living on little but that milk. And it was as sweet and rich and plentiful as ever. Who was feeding the beast? And better than I?

When I had drunk I would lean back in the straw, against the wall by the door, and watch my own thin blade set behind me, in the shadow. I would sit and watch the black clover growing in the sky. I would watch.

An Awakening

ALL DAY the wintry sun had hung in the same place.
It went out slowly, there behind its curtains. It
was gone then, and I was on the hill just as so often before, walking on, and nothing had changed. A gradual
climb but a long one. Lit by memory, at that hour: the
gray visibility addressing me from little stones, from the
tracks of the road, from the bushes and trees holding
themselves up like newspapers being read from the other
side.

How many days had I been on the way there? How
many days since the last time? Far be it from me to pretend I could answer. Far be it from me, I might have
said, to pretend to measure the present in terms of the
recurring past, but such a reply might not have been ac-
ceptable. Fortunately those questions were not put. No,
but it was not to be as I remembered it. I could see that
before I had gone far at all. Not something new, then,
but something that I was only this time coming to see,
though it had been there all the time. It must have been
there, now that I consider it, and I must have stared at it
again and again; gazed—with vacant eyes. No use re-

proaching myself: our time had come and it was beginning to appear to me at last. Like the lighting of a light. Three lights. Three figures coming toward me, stepping down, with baskets on their shoulders.

The first was a child with a basket of leaves. Gold light rose from them like the glow of a lantern, and as silent. The swarming leaves stirred as they rode, and the light rose out of them like breath. And the boy must have been there whenever I had been. Perhaps even before me, to judge by his clothes, which looked like those of boys in paintings from before my grandfather was born.

The next was a man with a basket of apples that gave off the same light. To think that I could have seen him and seen him (his clothes too from a generation long before mine) and never known. Perhaps because the glow from his basket was hard to distinguish from the fire in the sky behind him as he stepped toward me.

The last was an old man—how could I have missed such evidence of years combined with such strength? He was the tallest of the three, dressed for Sunday, and carrying a basket full of flames. Far down among them I could see a face lying. It would have been looking upward if its eyes had been open. Even among the flames its color still showed something of the old memory-gray. It might have been my own face which until then had seen nothing, being borne away.

When I looked up the night was over. There beside the road, as the sky whitened, I could make out the three baskets. No one was carrying them. A little smoke rose out of each of them. And a faint singing, dying away. In the smoke of the last basket I could see the same face, with its eyes closed, that had been lying in the flames. Its lips now were forming words to the song, but I could not make them out, though I drew close, and put my ear to the smoke, and shut my eyes. When I opened them to see where the music had gone, because I wanted to keep it, and form the words to it, there was the pale sun once more, hanging in a new place, for it will not be winter forever.

The Egg

FILLED with joyful longing I ran across the echoing
flagstone terrace and down the broad dressed-stone
steps, gradual as a beach, patterned with frost. The sky
was an immeasurable shell of shadow. The darkness of
the mid-winter season, when the sun never rises but the
land never goes out entirely, lay ahead of me, and the
empty plains, with thoughts rising out of the sleeping
snow, turning to look, reeling, running a few steps, falling again. Far beyond them, the Orphans' Gate. I carried the egg in my left hand, inside the glove, keeping it
warm. It meant that I had only one hand to do everything. To hold on. To wave. To fight. To balance. It
meant that I would have to let one thing go before I
could take up another. I had given up half of myself to
hold the egg. And the other half to the journey.

At the foot of the stairs, barely stirring in the twilight,
the dog teams were waiting, scores of them, lying in
harness, curled on the packed snow. Beside each of them
was the driver's round skin tent, and the driver himself,
walking up and down to keep warm. Here and there, to
what looked like a great distance, fires were fluttering in
silence, like votive lights in a cathedral, with dark furred

figures huddled near them. As I approached a team its driver would step toward me, grinning fiercely to show what a formidable personage he was, waving his arms to make me realize how he cracked his whip, how he terrified his dogs, how his sled flew on, how the Tooth Spirits, the Eye Spirits, the Hand Spirits, the Bear Evils, the Wolf Evils, the Crow Evils, the Knife-Carrying Ghosts, the Ice-Hollow Ghosts, the Sinew Ghosts, the robbers, and the very stars of wrong courses fled from him. He would open his mouth to show how his voice went out ahead of him to tear into his team like the heat of a building burning behind them. The whips were cracked only in gesture and no voices came from the drivers' mouths, for fear of waking the dogs. I passed driver after driver, each more awesome than the last, each offering me, on his palm, the little bell that was his life—mine for the journey, to return to him only if he brought me safely to the Gate. But I knew not to choose any of these. Ages ago when the first of my kind gave up part of his balance, forever, to pick up a stone, which at once began to be something else, he was rewarded with knowledge. I looked through the crowd until I found, at the edge of the camp, a team of skinny dogs piled in a heap, and a crippled driver limping beside his famished tent.

I stopped there and he hobbled up to me. Nothing about him was ingratiating. Besides being a cripple he had only one eye—his left. And the bell he offered me in his twisted palm was a piece of ice. His sled itself was built with one side different from the other. As I was, now. I nodded my head and he gave a little whistle and the dogs began to stir. And as they did I thought I could feel a stirring in the egg, in my palm—a turning inside it, or even the first faint vibrations of a cry. And once again in my mind I saw—but more clearly than before—the towering columns and the low door of the Orphans'

Gate, where no one would know me, but where they would recognize the egg that my mother (who was an orphan) had given to me, and would let me pass through to where it would hatch out and fly before me, pausing, hovering, calling its icy song.

The Herald

A FTER his death the herald was led into a place of
stone, as he could tell from the texture of the
cold on the soles of his feet, by the brushing of the cold
against his cheeks and his forehead, by the taste of the
cold, and by the smell of water that had turned to stone
—a smell that he remembered, and with pleasure, out of
some sunny morning at the beginning of his childhood,
though he could not remember what it had been doing
there. He had been lying alone, wrapped in white, in a
bright room filled with breezes and with silent birds of
reflected light. These had shimmered on the cool whiteness that was folded around him and still contained the
presence of the hands that had tucked him in and had
caressed his forehead, before leaving like part of a
shadow. And the birds of light had shimmered on the
cool whiteness that formed the next shell around him,
which was made up of the walls and ceiling of the airy
room. They joined the concentric spheres. It had been
a moment of happiness, in which the smell of water
turned to stone had passed like a white fish, never looking at him, and he had laughed to himself, without even
knowing that he was born.

So after his death he was led into a place of stone, as he could tell by the fingers of cold, and by the long clothes of the cold passing near him, and by the breath of the cold in his ears, and by many other signs at once, and the blindfold was removed. He was standing in a huge hall of stone. The shallow vaults of the ceiling looked so low that he imagined he could touch them, but he felt that to do so, even to raise his arm, would be a terrible act. He turned slowly. The echo of the last crashing note of a trumpet kept dying away, dying away. The hall appeared to be an enormous circle, but he could not see whether the vaults and the floor ever met. As he turned he saw that stairs led up out of the hall at intervals, all the way around: curving stone staircases, and on each of them the shadow of a man blowing a trumpet was just disappearing around the corner as he looked. He turned more quickly, in order to look behind him, and it was the same. But the dying echo came from none of the stairs. It came from the stones. He stopped turning and at once the whole of the hall was visible to him, on all sides. The echo faded out. The black shadow flag hanging from the black shadow trumpet disappeared from all the stairs. Then the hall filled with a rush of silent birds of light, and among them the herald floated like a white fish borne up by distant laughter. He floated there without moving, at last, and was the will of the king.

The First Time

I T WAS the first time. So it was terribly windy. And
of course he had no clothes. If you see someone with
clothes you know it is not the first time.

So he stood there in that time with no clothes and he
was not complaining because how should he complain:
he did not know that anything else was possible. The
wind tore the tears from his eyes. If he had not been
naked there would have been no light at all. A long moan
streamed from him but there was no way of telling
whether it came from his mouth or was a sound made
by the wind falling from him like a climber from a cliff.
As for him he shivered with cold. He trembled with fear,
for like most mortal creatures he could tell that the abyss
was never more than a step from him. He shook as we
all do when we are leaves.

Then she said to him, "It is a place of passage."

Then she said to him, "In places of passage it is always
terribly windy."

Then she said to him, "When you are in the places of
passage stop trembling and the wind will wait outside."

At last he slept. It was the first time that he slept in
that form, with all the forms behind him still waiting,

and all the forms ahead of him still waiting, each in its own way, silent, and untouched by wind. And the wind slept at his feet like a garment he did not need. The whole sky slept at his feet like a black garment. Like a garment he did not need for the first time.

She never left him.

But each time he sleeps he wakes missing something else for the first time, some limb, some knowledge, some part of him, and he sets out in a place of passage, looking for it for the first time, naked, not even knowing what it is, unable to see for darkness and tears. And the wind is terrible. And again he will have to sleep in order to find what is missing.

The Fragments

I AM beginning at last to have moments when something tells me of the miracle. I can be no more specific than that. Not yet.

I suppose I could be called grateful. Things were worse before. Before there were any such intimations. I can't take credit for the difference. I don't think I can take credit for it.

Certainly it was worse when I first came into the high room and found, in the middle of the table, the hand. All by itself. Palm up. Clean. Empty. Apparently. Like one of my own but without the scars. As I noticed in due course. Motionless but otherwise with nothing to indicate death. Warm. As I learned in due course. No sign of violence: no blood or bruise. Where it ended, where one would suppose that it had joined a wrist, after the manner of its kind, there was no garish explosion of reds, blues, yellows, no jumble of bared bone, of tubing severed in mid-syllable, of sinews shrinking. None of that. An oval segment of some colorless background, as it were of a foggy winter day in which one cannot make out details but only the day itself. I did not touch it.

It offered no explanation. Well, a hand does not offer

explanations. For being a hand. Even when one knows
how much is at stake. Thinks one knows. What is all
that, all that is at stake from our point of view, to hands
when they are on their own? But I had never thought of
that. So I stood there convinced that I understood nothing, which was a help for a while. I watched it, sure that
it knew something. Something, therefore, which I didn't
know. Many things which I didn't know. My assumptions about the nature of knowledge, I realized, were being shaken.

What was it for? Yes, I realized after a time that this
was the question I had been asking since the beginning.
No, not asking: embodying. Once I recognized that,
things became a little clearer. I saw that the hand was
not still, as I had at first imagined. For I had thought at
first, in my self-centered way, that the hand was motionless whereas I, by contrast, was moving. Now it
seemed to me that I was standing as a single spot in a
progression too vast for me to even imagine more than a
section of it, a progression which represented the story
of the hand, the destiny in whose service the hand had
come to decision after decision, millions of years before
I had been heard of, in order to lie, for however long,
where it now lay, in its present form. Then I saw it as a
path on which I was allowed to take only one step. A
path which knew its origins, its end, its purpose between
them—or at least more of these than I could guess.

Night fell. I let it fall around the hand, and I left. The
next day the place was empty and I embarked on the
usual doubts, as I still do. There was no proof. Nothing
else seemed to have changed.

So things went on in the old way until the day when
I came in as before and in the same place found the ear.
Empty. As far as I could tell. But I was careful to make
no noise. Detached like the hand. Same reflections in
my mind. Turning around how much it knew, apart from

me, if such a thing were conceivable. What decisions of its own were leading it past me, even as I watched? I began to think of myself as an instance. And the ear—what was it on its way to hear?

Then the ankle, the hair, the tongue. What am I but a caravanserai whose very walls belong to the camel-drivers?

Five thousand had come to hear him, and some had travelled a long way and were hungry. What was there for them to eat? One of those who were with him said, "There is a boy here with five loaves and two little fish, but what are they among so many?" But he said, "Let them be given to everyone who is hungry." And when everyone had eaten his fill the fragments were gathered up and they filled twelve baskets.

I mention this because when I found the tongue it came to me for the first time that the miracle was not the matter of quantity but the fact that the event had never left the present. Parts of it keep appearing. I have begun to have glimpses of what I am doing, crossing the place where they have all been satisfied, and still finding fragment after fragment.

Dawn Comes to Its Mountain in the Brain

There the east, the rim, is somewhere in the center, an area like another, in appearance. But in appearance it is all in the dark. In appearance it is all imprisoned in a night without stars. Nothing is more silent than those valleys that are the cradles of the voices. Nothing is more oppressive than their sky.

Then on the slope that contains the east there is a stirring. In appearance it would be said to dilate, break, scatter slowly, sinking, dwindling, reappearing, like the spots of color on the skin of a dying squid. But the spots do not die. They become more intense, they merge. All in utter darkness.

Now in the valley beyond, under the eyes of invisible horsemen, long baggage trains are trickling away, the drivers hastily lashing down the covers of the wagons as they go. Those tribesmen will never have names. Some of them will return. None will be forgotten. In the valley beyond that one, unseen herds vanish among the rocks, without a sound.

The stain deepens on the slope. It gathers. Settles. Like the playing of lights. But all this in a darkness like the darkness in wires through which a message is flowing.

Like the darkness around the queen in a hive to which a message is coming. Like the darkness in which justice is shown her palaces. And in a silence like that around a wire through which a message is passing.

It is only inside that slope that the trumpets sound, the processions and their watchful horsemen are seen departing, the last echoes of the herds fade out, and the sun rises with its message: Sun.

The west is in the same place.

About the Author

W. S. MERWIN was born in New York City in 1927 and grew up in New Jersey and Pennsylvania. He worked as a tutor in France, Portugal, and Majorca, and has translated from French, Spanish, Latin, and Portuguese. He has published more than a dozen volumes of original poetry and several volumes of prose, including his memoir of life in the south of France, *The Lost Upland*, and a new book of poems, *Travels*. He has been the recipient of a PEN Translation Prize, the Fellowship of the Academy of American Poets, the Bollingen Prize, and the Pulitzer Prize, among many others. He lives in Hawaii and is active in environmental causes.